The Storms of God

In Loving Memory

"Amazing" Grace Elizabeth

Table of Contents

Part I

The Hail Storms of God

Satchel, The Legend

The rocks of rain that fell on the earth this day had finally ceased. The tribe lived on this land for hundreds of years and they were familiar with the storms. They lived in tented homes and remained unto themselves. They were a close knit group, and survivors of the pillage of Indians across the land. Only thirty-nine remained.

Malina turned to Poncho and said while folding clothes, "Satchel is growing faster by the day."

"Yes my love, he's strong." He answered as he kissed his wife's cheek.

"Mama, Satchel is teasing me." Mya screamed while running in the tent.

Malina went outside the tent and there was Satchel playing with the other children.

"Satchel, Dinner is ready."

Satchel came to the place where he and his family sat around the campfire to eat their meals.

"Satchel stop teasing your sister." Malina said as she, Poncho, and Mya came out of the tent.

"Ma, I just told her to get out of the way. I, Sand water, and River were playing with the rain rocks and she was in the way."

"Satchel be kind to your sister." His mother insisted.

"Yes, Satchel be kind to your sister or tomorrow you and I will not go on your first hunt." Poncho interrupted.

"I'm sorry Malina." Satchel replied with those hazy black purple eyes. "I can't wait!" he continued.

"Your first hunting lesson." Poncho said with pride.

"Father, do you remember your first hunted meal?" Satchel asked with excitement.

"It was a raccoon. I remember my father taking me and showing me how to use my bow and arrow. I spied in on the furry animal and with great precision I released my bow. We had roasted raccoon. I had become a man." Poncho replied.

"I can't wait!"

That evening Satchel, his family and the other members of the tribe sat around the campfire, eating and talking. Satchel had grew knowing only the members of the tribe. Everything he knew he learned from his tribe. The next morning Satchel arose early. He was dressed and waiting on his father outside the tent.

"Ok son, you have your bow and arrow?" Poncho asked walking out of the tent.

"Yes"

"Very good! Seems you have learned the first lesson. You can't hunt your prey without your weapons in hand. Now, do you think you remember the lessons of how to use your weapons?" Poncho asked.

"Father, I remember everything you have taught me."

"We will see. Nothing like a hunt to test a man's knowledge and instinct. It doesn't matter if you are the hunter or the hunted." Poncho replied.

The two walked quietly for miles in the forest looking for their prey. Poncho had taught Satchel that when you hunt you walk with stillness like the trees. They walked and suddenly the prey appeared. Poncho signaled for Satchel to get his bow and arrow ready; however, Satchel

had already locked his eyes on the animal. Satchel raised his arm and eyed his prey. With a still hand, Satchel released his arrow and killed the possum.

"I did it father!" Satchel whispered with excitement.

"You can speak up now. The possum is dead." Poncho chuckled. I see you're going to make a great hunter. You will be able to provide well for your family one day." Poncho said while patting Satchel's left arm.

The two walked back to the camp. When Satchel saw the camp fire he ran to the others. All the men gathered around Satchel and with his spoil lifted him in the air. He had made an important step into manhood. That night the family had possum and Poncho looked proudly into his son's eyes.

After dinner Satchel would take his usual walk up to the pond and visit his friend turtle to tell him of his great day. He had known turtle since he was three years old. He and his mother would sit watching the calm of the pond and a small turtle would slowly crawl up and sit beside him. Ever since, Satchel had considered the turtle his pet animal.

For the next three years, Satchel would continue to learn the customs, beliefs, rituals, secrets, and the heart of his people. As Satchel's hunting lessons became more difficult, his ventures had now taken him to the secret parts of the forest which led to an unusual discovery one day. Poncho and Satchel were hunting one day when Satchel tripped and fell over a small door handle on the earth's floor covered with leaves.

"Be careful Satchel of the door." Poncho said.

"What is this father?"

"Well I guess you are old enough to know. If I tell you something you must promise to keep the secret of this land. "

"What secret?"

"Sometimes we tribe members lead others who pass through to freedom. "

"Where does it lead?"

"To the other side." Poncho smiled.

"I don't understand." Satchel said with much confusion.

"This passageway is used by slaves."

"Have you ever seen them?"

"I remember one night there was a run- a-way slave who came through our land. He was a dark purple man who was as tall as the sky and glistened like snow. Well the chief elders did not know what to do except to lead him to our tunnel. We told him to follow the tunnel straight through and he would be on the other side of the land. Ever since then, this way has been a passageway for slaves." Poncho replied looking up in the sky.

"Can I help?"

"No son, you are still too young. Remember this is dangerous."

"Why do we help?"

"There is nothing worse for a man than to be a slave. For to be a slave is to be dead."

"Who made the tunnel?"

"Our ancestors built this passageway from the great storms that would come to this land. The hail that falls on us now is nothing like what we used to see. I remember a great storm when I was a small boy. The tribe had to stay in this tunnel for days." Poncho said as he reminisced about the storm.

"What is hail?" Satchel asked.

"They are what you call your rain rocks." Poncho smiled. "We better get going. Dinner will be ready door." Poncho continued.

"Ok father."

"Remember Satchel, this must be kept secret. Not even Sand water or River must know."

"Yes father. "

"You know son it is strange you would trip on the door handle. I had a dream the other night that I was looking down and I saw you as a chief elder of the land."

"Dad, just let me enjoy my rabbit for tonight."

"Of course." Poncho laughed.

Another three years had passed and Satchel had become a strong young man and an excellent hunter. Satchel had not only learned to hunt his prey, but skinned the animal. One morning, Satchel decided this would be the day he would arise early before everyone else and go hunting for a special meal for dinner tonight. Today was his father's thirty-third birthday and he wanted to surprise the camp with a great meal. Usually he would not go alone but he knew the land well and hoped to be back before everyone awoken.

When Satchel walked away this time something seemed different. He turned back to see the camp and still no one had arose. He had a funny feeling but nothing could prepare him for this day. He thought maybe he was excited about his hunt. He wanted to wake Sand water and River to go with him but he did not want them to get in any trouble. Today he went to the farthest side of the land. He had drifted off thinking about his future only to realize there was a tiger staring at him. He had not heard anything and so at that moment he stood with great stillness. The tiger snarled walking towards Satchel. Satchel slowly raised his bow and arrow and with excellent archery he released his bow. Satchel could only think this is going to be a great dinner tonight. After skinning the tiger and cutting the meat, Satchel walked back to the camp not realizing how long he had been gone or how far he had gone. He could only think of the great distress his mother would be in when she awoke and did not find him this morning. As he approached the camp, he thought of what his punishment may be; however, something was different and very wrong as all he saw was a ripping fire of their tents. Satchel looked in despair and before he knew it he dropped the tiger meat to the ground and ran as fast as he could to the camp. What he saw would change his life.

Never had he seen the earth's ground so red. The chief Elders, River, Sand water, and the entire tribe had been shot with the white man's gun. Satchel looked desperately for his family and there was his sister and mother clutched in each other's arms covered in blood. Then Satchel eyes fell on his father Poncho and Poncho eyes looked at Satchel.

"Father!" Satchel yelled.

"Now son, calm down and listen to me. The white men came through here looking for a run- a-way slave. We told them nothing. So they left our bodies to be food for the animals."

"Father, no!" Satchel cried.

"Satchel, listen. I love you. You will be the hope of our tribe. You are now the chief elder of the land." Poncho said as he touched Satchel's face with all the strength of his left hand. "Continue our ways and remember we will always live in you. "

"Father, you can't die."

"Satchel there is a secret in the tunnel. There is a bag. "Poncho's last words as he breathed his last breath and dropped his hand with his eyes affixed on Poncho.

"Father, what secret is in the tunnel? Father don't leave me. Father! Father!" Poncho screamed with a chilling cry but it was too late. As Satchel's tears fell to the earth, the rain rocks came beating upon Satchel and the crimson red drenched bodies of his tribe.

The next morning Satchel dried his tears. He did not know what to do. He was confused, hurt, and alone. Despite everything he would have to bury the bodies. Satchel managed to begin to cut the small trees and band them together. It seemed he had worked for days making rafts but it had only been a few hours.

Satchel thought "How on earth was he going to carry these bodies to the river?" He had decided not to think of that now and to continue to make the rafts. On the second night after the massacre, the worst hail storm in years had come to the land. It must have hailed for hours. Satchel had to take cover in the farthest of the trees in the forest. Satchel cried as he wondered why God had left him alone and that is when he heard a voice.

"Hey, boy can you help me find the men who know of the tunnel."

"Who is that?"

"Hey boy, look over here." A voice said when Satchel laid eyes on the black figure standing out from a tree. It was a slave.

"The other day white men killed my tribe while I was hunting in the forest. But. "

"But what?"

"I know where the tunnel is."

"My God. Do you think the white men know where the tunnel is?"

"No, my father assured me before he died they said nothing."

"What you doing now boy?"

"Preparing for the burial of my tribe."

"Can you lead me to the tunnel?"

"I will show you the tunnel if you help me bury my tribe."

"I can't do that. If I am caught you and I are both dead."

"That doesn't matter to me. I have nothing left. It is up to you if you want to help." Satchel said as the hail storm had ceased.

"You promise to show me the tunnel if I help you?"

"I promise." Satchel replied.

That night in the dark the biggest burly black man Satchel had ever seen worked fiercely by the light of the moon. The wooden raft floats to lay the bodies had been made and their surface was covered with small pine trees. One by one Satchel and the slave carried body after body from the camp to the river. Satchel helped picked up the bodies of his chief elders, his friends, his sister, his mother and father. Satchel and the slave lay the bodies on the rafts according to their family name. Wooden raft after wooden raft of bodies were pushed out in the river and Satchel having made fire by wood lit each raft.

Satchel stood with tears in his eyes as he watched the rafts one by one burn with the people he loved.

"You all right boy."

"Yes."

"Hey boy we have two dead soldiers at the camp. What are we going to do with them?"

"Throw their bodies in the river." Satchel said walking away.

After Satchel and the slave threw the last body in the river the slave stood still for a moment to ponder what happened this nightfall.

"Boy, why don't you come with me."

"No, I am going to honor my father's wishes. I will lead you and others to the tunnel. I am not running from this land for anyone. This is my land."

"Ok boy, you a crazy Indian."

"Follow me to the tunnel quickly. Daylight will be here soon."

"Boy, what is your name?" the slave asked as he stopped walking.

"Satchel."

"My name is Jacob. Look here boy, take this. It is all I have." Jacob said standing with a gold ring in his right hand.

"What is this?"

"It's a gold ring. Don't ask how I got it, but it is yours. Take it."

"I can't take it. Besides you just helped me bury the dead in my life." Satchel sighed.

"This night you buried your friends, your family and even with all you loss you remain here to honor your people and help us slaves.

Take it, please." Jacob begged as he gave the ring to Satchel. Satchel held the gold ring and looked at it seeing his own reflection.

"Well, show me the way so I can get going?" Jacob said.

Satchel continued into the forest showing Jacob the handle of the door of the tunnel. Jacob looked back to Satchel and said "Boy I will pray God keep you and take care of yourself."

"I will."

From that day forward Satchel remained on the land helping run-a-way slaves find the tunnel. During these five years since the massacre of Satchel's tribe, he learned not only more about the land but the animals, trees, and plants of the forest. There was no inch of the forest that he did not know.

As always every morning by the river Satchel would stand for hours and watch the fog lay over the water. He smiled as he knew it was his ancestors watching over him. There were mornings he smiled remembering his friends and family and other mornings he would cry profusely. This morning Satchel did neither. He realized how the years had passed while looking at his reflection in the river. He saw how much he had changed. Satchel was much taller, his legs were much bigger, and his arms were much stronger. For the first time Satchel saw himself as a man. He had come to realize the events in his life had overcome his innocence as a boy. For the past five years he had battle the war of loneliness in his mind, the perils of despair in his heart, and the ambivalence of how he came to know God in his soul. While these thoughts raced through his mind, he was frightened as he turned from his reflection to see an image standing behind him.

"Don't be frightened." A soft voice spoke.

Satchel looked at the figure with a mysterious curiosity. Satchel had never seen a white woman. Her skin was olive with her big brown eyes and black hair. He thought to himself it would only be a matter of time before the white man would come and kill him.

"My name is Ariel. I'm a run-a-way slave."

"What on earth was standing before him?" Satchel questioned. He had never seen a white run-a-way slave.

"Do they have white women as slaves?" Satchel asked.

"Well, no. I am a Negro. I just look white. My father is the master of the plantation where I am from and my mother is a slave maid. I just look more like my father, then my mother."

"Why are you here?"

"My master's wife was getting more jealous of me by the day. So I ran here to find the tunnel."

"What makes you think I know of this tunnel?"

"Indian boy you are best kept secret among negro slaves. You are our secret of hope. Do you think you could show me the tunnel?"

"As far as I am concerned, I have no idea what on earth you are talking about white woman."

"Look, really I am a slave. I know my skin looks white, but I promise you I am a Negro."

Satchel looked the woman up and down to notice her torn skirt and worn shoes. The woman looked back at him. Satchel walked past her and as she ran behind him. She pleaded for him to show her the way to the tunnel, but Satchel continued to walk forward. He stopped for just a second to look at the sky, and then he continued in a hurried pace toward his tent. As he walked, Ariel yelled "I am negro" while the wind began to blow fiercely. As

Satchel approached his tent, Ariel stopped ten feet behind him. She continued to yell "I am negro" in the storm and that is when lightning struck a tree. Ariel looked up with fear and stood trembling while the tree limb approached rapidly towards her. Satchel pushed her out the way only but not before the limb gashed his right leg. Satchel had fallen to the ground and the pain in his leg was unbearable. Ariel sat up in amazement realizing Satchel had not only saved her life but he was hurt. The blood from his leg seemed to run like the river and flowed like the hail that was now pounding the earth. Ariel stood up as she helped Satchel stand and walked over the fallen tree to his tent.

"Oh, my God. This is my fault. This is bad. " Ariel cried walking Satchel to the tent.

"I have some supplies over there." Satchel said pointing to his right."

Ariel was more scared than ever. Satchel was now unconscious and she had to do something and quick. She took the bandages and applied as much pressure to his leg wound as she could. After much time finally the bleeding slowed but now Ariel knew she had to clean the wound. She had seen many times the nurse maids clean the whipping wounds of slaves, but she had never cleaned the wounds herself. She did only what she could remember. She wondered how the Indian had so much. As she looked around the tent she saw knives, bottles of sab, bandages, blankets, silver candlesticks with candles, bags of cotton, and so much more. She dressed and bandage the wound and she could only hope Satchel would awakened soon.

Ariel sat by Satchel's side pondering for hours over the things she had endured the jealously of the other Negro slaves because she looked white and the jealousy of her master's wife because she was Negro. Master treated Ariel with sweetness and kindness, but she could feel the tension in the house as his wife had confronted her about possibly selling her to another plantation since her services were not needed. Master's daughter Emily was getting married soon and would be leaving to be the lady of another plantation that had more than enough slaves to do all the housework. So Ariel ran away as soon as possible leaving behind everyone, including Dubose. She thought of him as she ran away but time was of the essence. Besides, it would be hard for her to be with any Negro. She had grown up in the big house surrounded by the finest linens, food, and silver all her life. Even her hand me downs that came from her Master's daughter were better than what the slaves had. She traveled with the family on vacations as a playmate for Emily. She thought it was no need telling Dubose anything. She just knew she had to find the tunnel and then she would find and marry one of the whitest, richest men in the country. It would be another day before Satchel awakened to find Ariel by his side. When he woke he did not know if Ariel was the most beautiful creature he had ever seen or an exotic creature he should be careful not to touch. There she looked at him wiping his head with a wet cloth. While she wiped his forehead, Satchel was able to look at Ariel closely. He saw her delicate frame that was small in nature and her skin smooth as coconut.

"Thank God you are awake. You had a slight fever, but I think it is broken. I cleaned your wound and bandage it. Your leg will be fine." Ariel smiled.

"Thank you, White negro slave." Satchel said.

"So you do believe I am a slave."

"Maybe" Satchel said shrugging his left shoulder.

"Maybe after you feel better you can show me the tunnel."

"I must decide what to do. I don't know what to think of you."

"Well I know what to think of you. You are the Indian who saved my life. What is your name?"

"Satchel"

"Well Satchel, get some rest. We will talk more tomorrow." Ariel said.

When Satchel awakened the next morning he saw no one. He thought maybe Ariel had left. He was not surprise. He went to stand realizing his leg was much worse than what he thought. He lay back down to rese some more. Ariel was walking through the forest looking for the tunnel. She thought it had to be close to the tent in which the Indian lived when she heard a voice behind there. There stood a brown colored man.

"Dubose, what on earth are you doing here?" Ariel asked while running into Dubose's arms.

"Ariel, I knew you would come to this land. I should have never told you about it."

"Have you found the Indian?"

"Yes, but he thinks I am white."

"Really now!" Dubose laughed.

"Don't you tease me Dubose. Besides I have to stay a little longer. The Indian saved my life yesterday and hurt his leg."

"So what you doing in these forest?" Dubose asked.

"Getting him some water."

"I know you Ariel. You are looking for the tunnel. You are scared they are going to find you gone, but don't worry. Master left town this morning on business and Misses and Emily are shopping for wedding dress fabric. I don't think anyone has missed you since you always go to the pond and read in the mornings. "

"His name is Satchel." Ariel said.

"Who is Satchel?" Dubose asked.

"That's the Indian's name." Ariel replied.

"Well, show me the way to the Indian boy. Maybe I can get the answer out of him."

As Ariel showed Dubose to the tent, both entered while Satchel was trying to sit up.

"Let me help you Indian." Dubose said while helping Satchel sit up.

"Satchel, don't be scared. This is another run-a-way slave looking for the tunnel."

"Yes sir, my name is Dubose."

Satchel looked at Dubose and asked, "Do you two know each other?"

"Well we know of each other. We grew up on the same plantation but the misses here grew up in the big house."

"Is she white?" Satchel asked.

"Well her father is, but her mother is a slave. That makes her negro."

"I have never seen a white negro."

"Do you think you would be able to show me the passage way once you feel up to it. Or you can tell me how to get there?" Dubose asked.

"You two are going to have to wait for me to show you. I don't give directions to the tunnel to anyone."

The next two days passed and Satchel's fever would come and go. Ariel grew even more anxious while Dubose became worried and unwrap and cleaned Satchel's wound again.

"Is everything ok?" Satchel asked while Dubose was now bandaging his wound.

"Don't worry my friend. You are doing fine. I will stay with you. It seems as though the wound was deeper than expected. You just get some rest. I am going to go and find us supper for tonight."

Dubose went outside the tent to greet Ariel anxiously pacing back and forth.

"How much longer Dubose is this going to take? We need to be getting out of here."

"Let me remind you he is hurt because of you. Besides we can't leave him until he is well. He has done a lot for us slaves."

"Well some good that does us. We still have no idea where the tunnel is."

"Well I have cleaned and re-bandage the wound. You may not have gotten all the infection out of that leg. That wound was extremely deep. He should be better in a few days. "

"A few days! Dubose we need to get going now!" Ariel spoke anxiously.

"Look Ariel, everything is fine and besides the Indian boy is a myth even to most slaves. I am going to get some food for us for tonight.

I will be back soon. Don't you leave and go anywhere. I mean it."
Dubose spoke firmly while Ariel sighed.

That evening while Dubose went in search for food, Ariel knew this would be her chance to get directions to the tunnel. Ariel walked inside the tent walking seductively towards Satchel as she spoke.

"You know Satchel, legend has it if you are given a gift you will lead the slave to the freedom door. Well, I have a gift to give if you would just tell me where the tunnel is." As Satchel listened to Ariel's proposition she slowly began to unbutton her shirt. "

"I have heard you and Dubose talking when you both thought I was asleep. It seems like you and Dubose know each other quite well. Dubose loves you Ariel."

"Dubose has always been smitten with me. Besides we need to get going."

"Tomorrow evening I will show you both the way to the tunnel. Now button your shirt before Dubose comes back." Satchel said shaking his head shamelessly.

"Please, Satchel do not judge me. Besides I was thinking you alone on this land, you probably have never seen a woman's bosom. Don't you want to feel the warmth of a woman's bosom?" Ariel smiled.

"What makes you think I have not already felt the warmth of a woman's bosom?" Satchel laughed.

"You are not at all impressed with me."

"I am only impressed with a woman when she is first impressed I am a man. A man is much more than the frame of his body just like woman is much more than the warmth of her bosom." "You're an arrogant Indian." Ariel spoke with disgust.

"Ariel tomorrow night, and not before then, I will show you and Dubose the tunnel. Leave me alone about directions to the tunnel." Satchel replied.

That evening Satchel did his best to act as usual. He felt sorry for Dubose because he knew Dubose had left the plantation looking for Ariel, a woman who did not love him. The next morning Dubose made sure Satchel was comfortable and his leg was healing. While inspecting and re-bandaging the wound Satchel said, "I think tonight I will show you and Ariel the tunnel. You both need to be getting on."

"I think we need to stay with you for another day. Just to make sure you are fine."

"Dubose you are a good man. You know I heard you and Ariel talking one night. Dubose, why do you love her?" Satchel asked with a strange curiosity.

"Oh, I don't know. I just do."

"Why you ask?"

"Well, I was taught a woman who loves a man never leaves him and if she does leave it is because he has driven her away. Ariel got scared one night and ran off. She didn't even bother to come get you." Satchel said with a suspicious tone.

"You may not know it but Ariel is a little mixed up in the head. It is nothing I can't handle. Ariel loves me and I love her." Dubose smiled as he finished bandaging Satchel's leg and continued saying, "This leg is healing and looking good my Indian friend."

"Thank you my friend. One more thing Dubose I need to tell you. If things in life change between you and Ariel, and I am still here you can always come back to this land and live." Satchel said.

"Thanks Satchel for the offer." Dubose replied.

That night Satchel led Dubose and Ariel to the tunnel. Neither of them would have ever guessed the tunnel was a door located in the ground. As they departed, Dubose turned back and shook Satchel's hand. With Satchel watching, both made their way underground and the tunnel door closed. Satchel walked back through the forest that night pulling some ground leaves from the earth. Then he visited turtle by the pond and walked back to his tent tired and fatigued. He cleaned his wound again with the sab from the ground leaves and re-bandaged his leg. He thought of how Dubose had chased a woman who was so easy to love as well as so easy to hate. He prayed that God would protect not only Dubose's life but his heart. Satchel continued to sit in his tent that night remembering the last words of his father. From that day forward he knew his legend gave slaves the freedom to hope.

His legend proclaimed if you can get to this part of the land where hail falls and find the Indian, he would lead you to freedom tunnel. For some, this legend would remain only a legend. For some, this legend became truth during the next five years before the end of the civil war. Afterwards, it would be two years after the civil war that one would see or hear of the name "Satchel" again.

The Storms of God

Pre-Sequel

Dahlia had come to live on the land with other freedmen. She was born exactly fifteen years before the end of the civil war. Her mother had come to this land with her younger brothers and sisters. This had become a territory of now forty -four former slaves. Dahlia loved to take walks to the river she had found one day being adventurous. It was during these walks Dahlia thought about life now and in the past. She recalled how her former master would call her the devil because of her glistening black skin and gold fiery eyes. Even now Dahlia would tell her siblings she would curse them with her eyes and they would run away in fear. Dahlia laughed at such silly thoughts as she stood by the peaceful river. She thought what a beautiful place to meet God. She turned to look back and there behind her was Satchel. His feet were wet and his skin hot. Dahlia's gold fiery eyes grew in stature as she said, "Why it is you! You are the Indian man. I thought you were something made up." Satchel stared at Dahlia and said nothing.

"What is your name? Are you the Legend Satchel?"

Again Satchel said nothing. Suddenly in his hand he lifted his bow and arrow and over Dahlia's head the arrow hit a rabbit. Dahlia fell to the ground quickly. She realized she was not the prey but the rabbit that was fifty feet behind her. Satchel looked at Dahlia while he walked passed her to get his rabbit.

Dahlia stood up and began to walk behind him. "Are you the Legend Satchel? Please tell me your name?"

"Why should I?" Satchel responded.

"Why, it is just we all have heard of the Indian who lives on this land and in this forest but it has been quite some time since anyone has seen him. Since none of my people had seen you, we all assumed you were just a legend. Am I dreaming?"

At that moment Satchel stretched his arm out towards Dahlia and she touched his hands.

"Oh my God, look at you. You are not a legend. My name is Dahlia. D-A-H-L-I-A. Da-li-a"

"Why do you come to my river?"

"To talk to God. Besides, I like to see the fog that lies over it."

"This is not fog."

This is fog."

This is not fog."

"Then what is it?" Dahlia asked.

"This is the spirits of my people." Satchel said pointing to the hazy patch of clouds that lay over the river.

At that moment Satchel faced Dahlia with coldness in his eyes.

"Oh, I am sorry. If you like why don't you come to my home and have dinner with us tonight. You must get lonely being in this forest."

"Your home is not your home. This is my home. This is my land. I decided to let you and your people stay. During the war I just decided to move further in the forest."

"You know where we live?"

"Yes, to the east and then north. I could have burn your houses and people many moon nights. "

"Why have you never come to us? Why didn't you say something?"

"No reason." Satchel said walking into the forest.

"Can you read?" Dahlia asked walking behind Satchel.

"No."

"I can. I can teach you if you want?"

"I thought slaves couldn't read."

"Well before we were free my family had a good master who allowed us to read. Why all my brothers and sisters can read. Satchel picked up the rabbit and began to walk away.

"Oh, please don't go." Dahlia said as she ran behind Satchel with the rabbit in his hand. As Satchel walked faster and Dahlia could no longer keep up Dahlia stopped and stood to watch Satchel walk away.

"Satchel I will come every day to this river." Dahlia yelled while Satchel faded into the trees. Dahlia ran as fast as she could through the trees towards home. She approached her camp out of breath and excited. She ran into the house and said with excitement "Mother, guess what?"

"What Dahlia?" her mother turned stopping to lift her head from scrubbing the wooden kitchen floor."

At that moment Dahlia thought she better not say anything. Who would believe her?

"Well child, what is it?"

"Oh mother, I saw a beautiful bird. It was red. I believe a cardinal." Dahlia said gripping her hands tightly.

"Why you stop my work to tell me of some bird. Dahlia get the water boiling and help me begin supper."

"Yes Mam."

"You the silliest child I know. You always are looking at trees, birds, and the sky." Dahlia's mother said as she kept scrubbing the wooden floor.

"Yes Mam."

That night Dahlia kept thinking of Satchel. She thought of how beautiful he was. He was tall and his skin like the color of pecans. His hair was black as tar but flowed like silk. His eyes a dark purple and with it she could see his sadness. That night Dahlia prayed for God to watch over Satchel and she hoped to see him again.

For the next few weeks there was no sign of Satchel. Everyday Dahlia would go to the river with her book and wait on Satchel and every day she was disappointed. She had almost given up hope when one day as she sat by the river waiting it began to rain. Dahlia picked up her book and began to walk as fast as she could but suddenly the rain began to get heavier and heavier. In a few minutes it felt like rocks were being thrown against her body. She began to run but she trip and fell to the ground. Dahlia dropping her book began to look for it but couldn't see and suddenly she felt her body being lifted and she was taken under a tree covering of leaves. Within minutes the hail stopped. There her eyes looked up and she saw Satchel.

"Are you ok?" Satchel asked.

"Yes. What happened?"

"A small hail storm"

"Hail storm. Why I have never seen anything like that."

"On this land it happens on occasions. Nothing you can do but wait until it stops."

"Oh, Satchel where is my Bible?" Dahlia asked frantically.

Dahlia began to look for her bible frantically when Satchel lifted his arm with the Bible in hand."

"Oh, it's wet." Dahlia sulked.

"You have come every day to the river for me." Satchel said.

"You saw me? Why didn't you say something? Where were you? " Dahlia asked in frustration.

"Like Satchel said before, this is my land and no one knows it better." Satchel replied.

"You know I can still teach you to read. We can write on the ground until my Bible dries."

"Why do I need to read white man's words?"

"Satchel, words are not for the white man. They are for everyone. And besides Satchel you need a friend. This way you and I can have something in common."

"I don't need a friend."

"You must need a friend. You have watched me for weeks come to this river."

"Mmmmm" Satchel said murmuring something of his native tongue.

"Tomorrow by the river." Dahlia continued.

"I will think about it."

"See you then. I better be getting home." Dahlia said as she ran away only to trip and fall again. This time she got up with her wet book in hand."

"Take your time Dahlia." Satchel said shaking his head slowly.

"I will." Dahlia said with an embarrassing smiled.

Satchel walked away into the forest. He followed Dahlia home and made sure she did not fall again. He thought Dahlia was energetic and smart, but quite clumsy.

The next day when Dahlia arrived at the river there was Satchel.

"Satchel" Dahlia said running to Satchel and hugging him by surprise.

"Dahlia, please control yourself." Satchel said pushing her away.

"It is good to see you. I thought I will start teaching you the alphabets and their sounds."

As she wrote with a small stick in the ground and the two bend over to see the writing Dahlia said, "This is A."

"A" Satchel said.

"Satchel, what is that scar on your leg?" Dahlia asked noticing his left leg.

"It is nothing. It is an old war injury." Satchel replied.

"Did you get hurt fighting the confederates?"

"No. I was trying to save a woman and let's just say all hell broke loose." Satchel laughed. "Now Dahlia, show me another letter."

From that moment Satchel and Dahlia would meet every day by the river for the next year learning to read and write. Satchel grew fond of Dahlia. One day the two took a break from their study and Satchel and Dahlia walked through the forest.

"I will call you "Yellow Moon"." Satchel said decisively.

"Satchel, my name is Dahlia."

"I know, but I will call you "Yellow Moon"."

"Ok. So what do I call you?"

"Satchel"

"Why will you call me Yellow Moon?"

"I call you not by your given name, but by the name of your spirit. You are Yellow Moon. You are different than any light in the darkness and you shine brightest."

"Well Satchel, Yellow Moon I am to you."

"Satchel, why are you called Satchel?"

"It is my Satchel that holds the future for others. My father said he could see that in me when I was born."

"I told you their spirits live over the river."

"Did you have any brothers or sisters?"

"At one time, but Yellow Moon I wish not to speak of my family."

"I won't ask any more about them, but if ever you want to talk about them, you can."

"Well, Yellow Moon this is where we go our separate ways for the day and night."

"Yes, see you again tomorrow Satchel."

"See you again tomorrow." And there Satchel stood at the edge of the forest watching Yellow Moon and he thought what a lovely spirit she had.

It would be that night that Satchel would sleep by the pond that lay to the back of the freedmen homes. "Turtle, I believe I have found a true friend this time. Maybe this time God will be kind to me." Satchel said to the turtle.

The next morning softness was in the air and again the spirits fell over the river. As Yellow Moon walked to the river she could see Satchel.

"Hello Satchel."

"Hello, Yellow Moon." Satchel said holding her hand. "Let us take a walk again today towards your home and talk."

"Ok."

"Yellow Moon I have been thinking and I have decided; if you agree, you should be my wife."

"Satchel, why I never gave it much thought." Dahlia answered amazingly.

"I know Yellow Moon. I am an older, wiser man. But I like your company and I have decided I don't want to be alone in this forest."

"Why Satchel, Have you ever had a love before?"

"Maybe, Maybe not! Besides it is of no importance since I want you to be my wife." Satchel replied sternly.

"Satchel, I haven't told anyone about you. My mother still thinks I just take time everyday looking at the sky and watching the birds."

"Yellow Moon of course I would ask your father for your hand in marriage."

"Satchel, my father is dead."

"Then I will ask your elders."

"Satchel we don't have elders."

"Then I will ask your mother."

"Satchel, I don't know about this. This is sudden."

"Do you have someone else Yellow Moon?" Satchel questioned.

"No, oh no, but Satchel this is a dream! All these years I thought you were just a legend only to discover you are a real man who wants to marry me."

"Yellow Moon, It is the softness of your heart where I want to lay my head and rest. Think about what I have asked today and give me your answer tomorrow."

"Tomorrow is rather soon, don't you think?" Yellow Moon replied.

"Tomorrow is ample time. Either you want to be my wife or you don't. It is that simple." replied Satchel."

"Tomorrow it is. I will have your answer then." Dahlia said with hesitation.

That night all Dahlia could think about was Satchel. First she did not know how she would tell the others of his existence, where they would live, or what a life they would have. She had so many questions and yet she knew deep in her heart she loved Satchel. He was kind and tenderhearted. She looked forward to their meetings by the river and she could not imagine another day without him.

The next day Dahlia did her chores as usual. It was just about time for her to meet Satchel and give him her answer. She was nervous and yet excited. She thought today she needed to be especially pretty. She picked a flower to place in her hair from the edge of the forest as she begun to take her journey. Suddenly Dahlia tripped and fell again. She thought how clumsy of her. She went to stand but her left ankle reeked with a bloody pain and she screamed. As she yelled for help Big Sammy looked to see Dahlia on the ground holding her ankle.

He ran over as fast as he could and said, "Ms. Dahlia what is wrong?"

"I think I may have broken my ankle."

"Oh, oh. Your mother will have a fit."

Sammy picked her up with his strong brawn arms and brought Dahlia back into the house.

"What's wrong?" Dahlia mother asked.

"Miss Dahlia done broke her leg. I will go and fetch the Doc."

"What on earth child have you done? I don't have time for this mess. I need you to help out around here."

Her mother just fussed and complained but Dahlia could only think how she needed to get to the river to see Satchel. If she had not been picking a flower and been so clumsy maybe she wouldn't be in this mess.

"And child what's that flower in your hair. " Her mother said snatching it out her head and throwing it out the window.

As her mother continued to fuss Doc came in the door and said, "Now mother Beasley calm down and let me take a look at the ankle."

The Doc examined her ankle said "Not so bad."

"Well, is it broken?"

"No Dahlia, it just a cut and a bad sprain. You will need to rest for a few days."

"A few days! Well I need her up and helping around the house." her mother chimed.

"Well that is impossible. She needs to stay off that ankle or you may not have her to help at all."

"Just look what you have done."

All Dahlia kept thinking as her mother hissed like a cat was how Satchel waited by the river and what he would think when she wouldn't come.

Satchel waited for Yellow Moon all that day. But there was no sign of her. He decided to never come back to the river again. It seemed to be the one place where everything in his life seemed to vanish. After a few days Dahlia was able to walk again and she made her way to the river but there was no Satchel. She waited as long as she could. She even yelled his name, but was answered by the echo of her own voice. She was in distress on what he must have been thinking.

For the next several days Dahlia went to the river but no Satchel. Her heart was saddened. She thought she would never see Satchel again. As the weeks passed, Dahlia still could not sleep. She tossed and turned but to no avail she could not rest. She thought of Satchel all the time and wondered if he was well. One night she gently arose from her bed not to wake the other children. She went to the door and sat on the stoop outside her house. She looked up at the bright stars and could see the moon. She thought what a beautiful night. She wondered where Satchel could be this evening. She wondered was he looking at the same sky she saw. Dahlia sat quietly for just a moment when she decided to take a walk around back. As she walked several hundreds of yards she could see the pond. She never took notice of the pond. She was so bewildered by the trees, the birds, and the sky somehow she overlook the calm and tranquility of the small pond. As she walked ever so softly she could see a shadow. Satchel suddenly appeared.

"Oh, Satchel" Dahlia said wanting to run into his arms but he refused. "I have looked all over for you. Where have you been?"

"What does it matter Yellow Moon?"

"You don't understand."

"I understand. I have been watching how that Sammy fellow looks at you. Is he your beau?"

"Sammy, that old goat! No." Dahlia giggled.

"So do you have someone else or you just don't like Satchel?"

"Satchel that day I was to meet you I fell and hurt my ankle. I couldn't walk for a few days. I went to the river as soon as I could but you never came."

"Sure Yellow Moon."

"Satchel, look I have a scar. Just like your scar."

While Dahlia showed Satchel her scarred ankle, he asked, "Yellow Moon what happened?"

"I was picking a flower to put in my hair so I could be pretty that day and I fell as I always do."

"So you were coming to see me?" Satchel asked.

"Yes Satchel. Oh Satchel, I will be your wife."

Satchel stood with the gentleness of a child as he looked into Yellow Moon's eye.

Then Satchel said, "It is settle. We will marry tomorrow. "

"Not so fast Satchel. I have to tell my mother about you. In fact I have to tell everyone about you. And where will we live?"

"We will live here on my land." Satchel said with his arms wide open.

"Satchel we need a home like the small home I have with my mother, and not a tent. "

"Well, then I will build you such a home tomorrow."

"I don't think you can build it in a day."

"I can. Your Satchel can do anything."

"I bet you can." Dahlia laughed.

"Tomorrow come out of this forest and meet my people."

"Ok" Satchel said and with the softness of her lips she kissed Satchel goodnight.

The next day as Dahlia and her mother washed clothes outside Dahlia looked for Satchel everywhere. She kept eyeing the edge of the forest but still no Satchel that morning. As she continued to wash clothes, Satchel appeared. He was handsome as he walked with certainty looking at her the entire time. Just as he walked out of the forest Sammy stopped chopping the wood and confronted Satchel.

"Sir who are you?" Sammy asked.

Dahlia knew this was trouble and dropped the clothes in the water barrel and ran towards Satchel as fast as she could but not before Satchel gave Sammy an upper right hook that laid him on the ground.

All the people stood in amazement and the men went to charge Satchel but not before Dahlia had made it into his arms.

"Dahlia, who is this?" someone asked.

"Look like an Indian to me." Another person said.

"Dahlia do you know him?" Sammy asked lifting his head from the ground.

"You better tell him to go away as we don't want any trouble." Someone said as the men had surrounded Satchel.

"Everyone Listen. This is Satchel."

"Now Dahlia, there is the legend about an Indian boy but no one knows for sure."

"No, the Indian boy has grown up and this is him. This is Satchel."

"All the men stood and glazed at Satchel and the women and children stared at a distance."

"I am Satchel." Satchel said pointing to himself.

"Well go away. We don't want any trouble." replied a five feet and four inch old man shaking his right index finger in Satchel's face.

"This is my land. You go away." Satchel groaned.

Dahlia's mother immediately rushed to Dahlia "Girl, look what trouble you have gotten us in."

"No mama, Satchel was here before us. He just never came to meet us. Why every day for the past year he and I have met by the river up yonder and I have taught him to read."

"Is this true?" her mother asked.

"Yes, Yellow Moon has taught me to read."

"Her name is Dahlia." Dahlia's mother said putting her hands on her hips.

"This is my land. I am the chief of this ground and her name is Yellow Moon and she is to be my wife." Satchel responded now putting his hands on his hips.

"Your what?" Dahlia's mother reeled.

"My wife"

"Dahlia, let's go in the house at once." Mother Beasley said grabbing her daughter and taking her in the house. The people just stood and stared at Satchel until a child asked, "Are you a real Indian?"

"Yes, I am. I am Satchel."

"Wow!"

"Johnny get away from him." as his mother grabbed the boy's arm. Meanwhile in the house Dahlia and her mother were having an unpleasant conversation.

"Look what has happened. This Indian thinks you suppose to marry him Dahlia."

"Mother I told him yes."

"You told him what!" Mother Beasley shouted.

"I love Satchel."

"Dahlia we don't know if there are more of them. They could kill us all."

"Satchel is the last of his tribe. And he could have killed us earlier but he didn't"

"Is everything all right?" Satchel asked stepping slowly in the house.

"Why Satchel, what you want with my daughter? Why she half cleans and cooks as it is and she is always tripping over things." Dahlia's mother said turning toward Satchel.

"I love Yellow Moon. She sees God in more places than anyone I have ever known."

"And if I decide I will not have my daughter marry you."

"Then as chief and owner of this land I will take her and marry her, of course if Yellow Moon wishes." Satchel smiled gazing into Yellow Moon's eyes.

Dahlia smiled in returned.

"Well since you love her so much where will you two live?

"We will live on the other side of the pond and live in my tent just until I have built Dahlia a house."

"Mm mm" Dahlia's mother groaned.

"Mm mm" Satchel groaned back.

"I will allow this marriage on one condition. You promise us people are safe on this land?"

"You are safe from me if that is what you are asking. You have always been safe from me." Satchel said with compassion.

"I don't know about this Dahlia." Her mother said with uncertainty.

"Oh, please mother. I am old enough."

Dahlia's mother paused for a few seconds and said with a hesitant smile, "Well ok."

"Then tomorrow evening before the sun sleeps Yellow Moon and I will marry by the river." Satchel said when Dahlia hugged her mother and then rushed into Satchel's arms.

"Now enough of that you too! We got a lot of work to do before tomorrow. I got to make a dress and a cake. Go on Satchel. See you tomorrow." Dahlia's mother said fanning her hand scatting Satchel away.

Satchel smiling at Dahlia as he walked out of the house.

Her mother looked at Dahlia she said "I am proud of my baby. Child you have hit a gold mine. Legend also has it there is gold in these parts and that Indian boy just may know where it is." Her mother said as she walked into the other room. "Well come on child so I can fit you for a wedding dress."

"Ma, I don't care about gold. I love Satchel."

"Stop talking so much. Come now and pulled out all our clothes from your dresser. I got to make you a wedding dress and a cake. I don't know how I am going to get it all done. Well I will just have to stay up all day and night. You are getting married." Dahlia's mother smiled.

Dahlia smiled in return and thought "Yes, I am."

It was the next evening just before the sun went down that Yellow Moon and Satchel were married by the river. Satchel took his knife and gently cut into his and Yellow Moon's arms and mingled their blood under the cloudy patchy haze over the river while the freedmen watch. Afterwards, they jumped over the broom as Yellow Moon insisted. Later on that evening, Satchel apologized to Sammy for the misunderstanding and Sammy said that was fine as he would have done the same. The two men eventually became the best of friends. That evening all the people gathered around a fire outside their homes and had dinner and for the first time in thirteen years Satchel thought just maybe God had wanted him to have a family on earth, again.

After dinner the crowd disappeared and Satchel and Yellow Moon went to their wedding tent Satchel had set up earlier that day talking about the day's events.

"I will build our home tomorrow." Satchel said while holding her in his arms.

"Just take your time, besides as long as I am with you I am home." Dahlia replied.

Satchel softly kissed Dahlia's lips when Dahlia said with hesitation "Satchel, I do want you to know something."

"What is that?"

"The only reason my mom let me marry you was because she thinks there is gold in these parts and you may know where it is."

"Your mother is right. There is gold on my land."

"Why Satchel you never told me? Where?" Dahlia asked with shock.

"I am looking at it." Satchel replied looking at Yellow Moon. Then they both began to laugh.

Satchel and Yellow Moon would go on to have six children: Poncho the Hawk, Jacob the Eagle, Sand water the Warrior, River the Stallion, Malina the Rose, and Mya the Hummingbird.

Part II

The Lightning Storms of God

Chapter 1

Death

Late in the afternoon when the sun reached the clouds, the rain began to pour over the old one story four-room house of Ma and Pa Whiting. Ma and Pa Whiting decided this even to sit on the porch, watch the rain, and take notice of God's voice. Pa Whiting was starring in the clouds as Ma Whiting was holding their two-year-old son Matthew in the rocking chair. Their six-year-old daughter Mattie was inside the house sleeping peacefully. The storm was fierce as usual and God's voice grew more thunderous. Lightning flashed and at first glance seemed to have struck about ten yards from the right side of the house.

The rain continued to poor and Pa Whiting was so entranced with the heavens he looked away for a moment and notice Ma Whiting slumped over in the rocking chair and Matthew shaking. He arose from his chair slowly and with great tremble. He walked just twenty slow steps to the right of his chair when he looked at his wife and noticed there was no more breath in her body. He reached for Matthew who had begun to make murmuring sounds. Pa Whiting looked to the heavens with Matthew in his arms and cried with the sound of falling raindrops. The thunder and lightning ceased at that moment.

And the day ended.

Chapter 2

Change

Within two days Mattie's mother had been buried under the big oak tree just fifty yards beyond the front of the house. Ma Whiting's sister, Lela, had come when she heard the news of her sister's death the next morning as Pa Whiting brought Matthew and Mattie to the reservation to see Dr. Williams. Lela lived on the reservation three miles west on the outer edge. The reservation had become the home of displaced Native American Indians, former slaves and first generation descendants of slaves. It was a community led by Chief Satchel where the hard work and struggles of Indians and Negros were evident and of course it was isolated from the rest of the world. On the land lay green grass, a small pasture, humming birds and oak trees so big that the tops of their tallest branches touch the sky.

The two -hundred people who lived on the land had come by way of the pillage, plunder, blood and death of their ancestors. Indians and Negros of all colors dwelled together and built an infrastructure of roads, buildings, homes, businesses, a school and church. The people were governed by men who were not elected by the people to lead but who assumed the position of leadership. Others who lived east ten miles away in the city thought the reservation was the worst place to live. The reservation was known for having treacherous storms over the five mile radius which the people lived. The small storms brought great rain, pounding thunder and shocks of lightning that could last for days. But too the people who lived on the land the storms became the way God spoke to them and how he directed their steps into their purpose.

Now Lela was able to convince Pa Whiting that Mattie should be in an environment with a woman in the home. She wanted to take care of Matthew but since Dr. Williams saw nothing wrong with the boy on examination Pa Whiting decided to keep Matthew.

Lela had been married for three years and had no children. Lela thought that just maybe God wanted her to rear Mattie as her daughter. Lela and Johnny had come to take Mattie just three days after the death of her mother. Mattie did not want to leave her Pa and Matthew but there was nothing she could do. Since the death of her mother, she had not spoken a word and showed no emotion.

Lela walked in Mattie and Matthew's room and she took Mattie by the hand while Johnny stood at the door with a small brown tattered suitcase. Matthew stood by crying and Pa Whiting stood with uncertainty and in a trance. Lela's voice seemed to be in a distance as she spoke to Mattie while walking her to the wagon. Lela explained to Mattie life on the reservation would not be all bad and how she would have dresses and be able to go to school. While Lela went on talking, Mattie looked back at Pa and Matthew. As she turned her head forward to face her future she remembered just a few days ago being awoken by rain when she got up and looked out the kitchen window. She saw her mother holding Matthew in the rocking chair. Her smiling mother turned to see Mattie through the window and then lighting struck and Mattie's eyes blinked. Her mother's eyes were closed.

The three mile ride to the reservation was long but when Mattie arrived she was surprised to see a few shops, grocer, café, homes, a school, and a church. Ma and Pa Whiting would only travel to the reservation for Christmas. She missed Ma, Pa, and Matthew already and could not decide whether to cry or enjoy all the colors she saw on the reservation. She was torn with so much emotion that she still could not speak.

"We're here." Johnny said. "I hope you like it. I finally finished the building on this house. Took me two years but it was worth it." Mattie showed no emotion as Johnny helped her step down from the wagon.   He then helped Lela from the wagon and picked up Mattie's suitcase. As they were walking to the front porch, Lela's neighbor Emma looked on.

"Is that the child, Lela?" Emma yelled from her front porch next door.

"Yes, it is." Lela replied.

"What's your name Baby?" Emma asked looking and smiling at Mattie.

Mattie looked at the short round stout lady and did not say a word.

"Is the child alright, Lela? Is she slow?" Emma asked with a suspecting tone.

"No, she is just sad about her mother. Her name is Mattie." Lela said with a quaint smile. Ms. Emma replied with a quaint smile and a head nod. It was then Mattie notice an Indian walking by and he waved to Johnny and Johnny waved back to him.

"Mattie that man is Satchel. His tribe was the first to live on the land. He is our eldest and most respected. Wave to him Mattie. "Lela said. Mattie waved to Satchel with a blank stare as she was mesmerized by his appearance.

 "Mattie, that man is the actual owner of this land. Rumor is Satchel was a young boy when Federal officers came and killed his tribe. He was the only survivor. He is married to a former slave and her name is Dahlia but we call her "Yellow Moon". You will get a chance to meet her later." Johnny spoke.

Satchel walked towards the porch standing on the last step.

"Good evening Satchel" Lela said.

"Good evening Lela. Hello to you Johnny." Satchel replied.

"Hello Satchel." Johnny responded.

"So this is the child you have been telling me about."

"Yes, Satchel. This is Mattie." Aunt Lela replied.

"Hello little one. I am Satchel."

While Mattie stood in silence Lela spoke out of awkwardness,

"Satchel, she is not speaking much today. I think Mattie is a little tired from her trip."

"I am sure she is tired. Don't worry Lela. Grieving takes time. She will speak when she's ready." Satchel smiled at Mattie.

"Yes, Satchel. Thank you for understanding." Lela responded.

"In the meantime, I will let you all get settle and tomorrow evening I will come by for the ceremonial blessing."

"Looking forward to it." Johnny said.

"Well I need to get going. I was just stopping by Emma's to drop of this sack of potatoes and then I have to go meet Dubose to his new horse."

"Good day Satchel." Lela spoke while Satchel nodded and walked away dropping off a bag of potatoes on Emma's porch.

Mattie just stared at Satchel. Even though she had visited the reservation before she had never seen Satchel. He stood with great stature with his built frame, hair touching the center of his back, high cheek bones and his mysterious blazing black purple eyes looked like fine silver.

As they entered, Mattie stepped into the covered screen porch. On the porch was a very nice table with the most beautiful of field flowers with a mahogany wood rocking chair on each side of the table. The chairs reminded her of the rocking chairs at home. After entering the porch, there was another door that led to inside of the home. The first thing Mattie noticed was the floors. Her shoes were so worn she could feel the wood beneath her. She entered the area where there was a table, mirror, and coat rack.

As Mattie looked around Johnny said "Let me show you what we have Mattie." He said pointing to the left, "Here are the family quarters. You can read here on this couch and write at this table and chair. Your Aunt Lela saw this red velvet couch and just had to have it. To the right he pointed and said "Here are the dining table quarters where we have Sunday dinner." It had a wood table and four chairs made from oak. Ahead of the family quarters to the left was Johnny's and Lela's room.

"This is your room Mattie." Lela said pointing to the wood door. "I know it isn't much. I hope you like it."

Mattie looked around and saw a small beautiful brass bed with the most beautiful of bed linen. In her room was a small table with a two drawers, mirror, and chair. Lela showed Mattie the closet where her new clothes hanged delicately on the fabric hangers. She had two dresses of cotton, a uniform dress, two shirts, a sweater, a nightgown, two pairs of shoes and undergarments. Mattie just looked in amazement. She wondered what on earth she would do with a dress. She had always worn coveralls.

"Of course you can keep your clothes if you want. I have some extra hangers."

Lela looked down at the child and noticed her shoes and said, "Looks like the shoes we have are just in time for you."

"Come and let's see the rest of the house."

They walked out of Mattie's new room and on the left was a room with a tub and washing sink.   They walked out of the bathroom into a small empty room. Down the center of the hall was a huge kitchen and Uncle Johnny showed Mattie the kitchen's working indoor water pump. It had a small table, four chairs, an oven, washing sink, and a few cabinets. To the back of the kitchen was another large empty room with an in house freezer and outside was the shed for the horse and wagon, a small chicken pen with four chickens, a small garden and an outhouse.

Mattie remained silent.

"Well I better let you girls get settle." Johnny said.

Lela took Mattie in her room and began to unpack her belongings. The first item Lela took from the suitcase was a lace handkerchief and Mattie took it from her hand only to hide it behind her back. Lela stood back to look at the child.

Lela smiled and said "Well, I see that is important to you so maybe you should put that in your drawer. "

Mattie turned slowly to her left and placed the small white lace handkerchief in one of the drawers.

Lela just smiled at Mattie as she continued to unpack her belongings.

"Let me take those overalls when you bathe tonight."

After bath time, Lela got Mattie's new cotton nightgown and helped her slip it over her head. She tucked Mattie in the bed and said this small prayer:

"Lord, this is me Lela and my niece Mattie. I thank you for her being here. Please watch over this house, land, and all who dwell in it. And Lord please let Mattie know how much her Uncle Johnny and I love her. Amen."

As Lela left the room, Mattie was thinking about Ma, Pa, and Matthew and how she missed them. Then she heard murmuring voices in the next room.

"Oh, Johnny I'm worried, do you think she will ever speak?" Lela asked.

"She will be fine dear. Just give the child time. This is a lot of change."

"Are you ok with this?"

"Yes, I know this will make you happy to have a child."

"Johnny I just want Mattie to know despite it all that maybe God wanted this.

"Everything will be fine. Let's go to sleep. I got to get up early in the morning and go to the mines." Johnny said holding Lela in his arms.

"Johnny, would it be ok if I quit my jobs?"

"Sweetie of course. You should have been at home anyway. I never wanted you to work. Besides I have taken another job keeping up the common areas of the reservation since Sammy died."

"Where will you find the time with you working in the mines?"

"I am man of this house. You just stay home and take care of Mattie. Besides you and I still have a nice nest egg. Now sweetie, go to sleep."

"Ok Johnny."

The next evening was Mattie's Ceremonial Blessing. Mattie stood in the center of the family living quarters while Lela and Johnny stood in silence. Satchel murmured words in his native tongue, danced around Mattie and wore his feathers on his head. As he performed the ritual Mattie thought how strange Satchel was behaving and yet Satchel was the most unique and strangest creature she had ever seen. While the ceremony proceeded Satchel looked in Mattie's eyes and said "Quiet Storm". Then Satchel left with Lela and Johnny looking at Mattie perplexed and bewildered by her given spiritual name. They dare not asked Satchel the meaning of this name. No one ever questioned Satchel. They just knew they would understand it all as time passed.

The next few weeks were different. Mattie had to get used to breakfast and dinner an hour later than usual. Lela took Mattie to the reservation school where she learned reading, writing, and arithmetic. Lela was able to quit both of her jobs and began to sit for two month old twin boys whose mother went to work at the reservation's cafe. Lela had managed to earn some money and still be home when Mattie arrived from school. The school was only a few blocks away and Mattie walked home alone. For weeks Mattie did not speak to anyone. The teacher assured Lela that Mattie would speak in her own time.

Pa and Matthew were coming to the reservation every other Sunday to have dinner. She and Matthew would play. Matthew spoke but with a stutter but Mattie still had not uttered a word. Each time Pa and Matthew would leave, Mattie would stare away.

One morning Mattie awakened. It was Saturday and as she lay in her bed she smelled food. She was hungry this morning. She leaped from her bed and put on her robe. As she came out of her room she walked to the kitchen and saw Johnny standing over Lela and the both of them standing over the wooden oven.

"What's that?" Mattie asked.

Lela and Johnny looked up and showed no unusual emotion.

"It is bacon from the grocer. We will be having it this morning with our breakfast. Wash up and change your clothes." Lela said.

Mattie walked away and went to the outhouse.

When she left, Lela looked at Johnny and said, "Finally."

"I told you sweetie not to worry. Is the bacon almost ready? It smells good."

"Breakfast will be ready in a few minutes. I suggest you go and wash up Johnny."

"Yes, Mam!"

Lela was relieved Mattie had spoken and that morning Mattie ate a good helping for breakfast. From that day every Saturday Lela cooked bacon. Mattie grew up with all the comforts her Aunt and Uncle could afford which were more than her Pa. She had the prettiest dresses made from beautiful fabrics and the prettiest wooden dolls.

After three years, Lela became pregnant. Lela and Johnny were shocked with Dr. Williams told them of the news. Mattie was sure she would be sent back to live with Pa and Matthew. She had grown to love the reservation despite the occasional lightning storms. But Mattie thought this baby would mean she would go back to the fields with Pa and Matthew.

This particular Saturday, Lela and Mattie were in the kitchen baking their usual Sunday cake. Mattie loved Saturdays because there was no school, she had her bacon and she knew her Aunt Lela would be baking a cake today. Mattie stood in the kitchen peering over the cake bowl and asked, "When will Pa come for me?" while dipping her finger in the left over cake batter Lela had place on the kitchen table.

"What do you mean?"

"When your baby come, I am going to have to go back."

"Go back where?"

"To live with Pa and Matthew again."

"You are not going anywhere. Your Pa agreed that Uncle Johnny and I would raise you as our own. Why Mattie you are going to become a big sister again."

Mattie smiled dipping her finger again in the left over cake batter. Mattie thought how nice it would be to have a little sister.

Chapter 3

Life

Fortunately Lela's pregnancy was very easy. She had a girl and they named her "Essie". Lela thought after caring for Mattie, God had decided to reward her. Another four years passed and Lela bore a son and they named him "Little Johnny".

Mattie's oldest cousin Essie thought for years Mattie and even Matthew were her older siblings. Though Essie could never figure out why Matthew did not live with them. Mattie was seventeen years of age and about to graduate the reservation school. Mattie had gone to the outhouse and when she returned to her room there was Essie looking at her new dress that hung from the inside of her bedroom door.

"Get out of here. You are always following me around." Mattie said as she pushed Essie to the side.

"Mattie do you like boys?"

"Why do you ask?" Mattie answered staring at her dress.

"Brock Williams wanted me to kiss him today so I could be his girlfriend. I told him I would have to ask my Ma."

"So ask her." Mattie shrugged.

"Ma is next door at Miss Emma's house so I thought I could ask you."

"Why are you asking me?" Mattie turned to Essie.

"Well you are my sister." Essie replied.

"Not really."

"What do you mean Mattie?" Essie asked.

"When I was little there was a lightning storm that killed my mother. Your Ma, my mother's sister and my Pa decided it would be best if I stay here on the reservation."

"Then, is Matthew my brother?" Essie asked as she put her finger to the tip of her mouth.

"No. Matthew and I are brother and sister and you and Little Johnny are our cousins."

"Why didn't Matthew and your Pa come to stay on the reservation?"

"My Pa wanted to stay on his own land and teach Matthew how to care for it. "

"Is that why you call your Pa "Pa" and my Pa "Uncle Johnny?"

"Yes, now get out of my room." Mattie said pushing Essie.

"Ok, ok." Essie said walking with her head down murmuring under her breath, "I still don't know whether I should kiss Brock Williams?
"

Mattie yelled out of her room, "No kissing Brock Williams and tell him he can go kiss a goat! "

The next morning Essie got a chicken out of the chicken pen and took it to school with her. Before school started she walked up to Brock Williams and said while holding the chicken firmly under her left arm,

"My sister Mattie told me to tell you I have no business kissing you and to kiss a goat. I don't have a goat but I have a chicken for you to kiss and you can make her your girlfriend."

Brock Williams became angry and threw a small rock at Essie as her and the chicken she held tightly ducked and he went running inside the school house crying to the teacher. The next few minutes, the teacher walked out of the school house with great steamed.

As she walked towards Essie, Essie said, "I told him I did not have a goat."

Without any questions, the teacher turned Essie around and hit her on her bottom with her ruler stick. Needless to say Essie got a spanking and Brock Williams' girlfriend, the chicken, got away.

That evening at supper time Lela said, "Johnny we are missing a chicken from the chicken pen."

Essie eyes got big as she stuffed a spoonful of mashed potatoes in her mouth."

"I don't think we have a thief on the reservation."

"Well you never know."

"If we are missing a chicken tomorrow, then the chicken probably got out somehow."

"You are probably right, Johnny."

That night Essie prayed her ma would not find out about her spanking at school and her stealing the chicken. The next morning when Essie got up for school something amazing had happened. Uncle Johnny came in the house telling Lela the chicken must have found its way back home. He had gone to the outhouse last night and heard it out running around in the yard. Essie thanked God for the chicken returning home and she promised never to ask Mattie about anything again.

Chapter 4

Love

After graduation from the reservation school, Mattie found a job working at the reservation's fabric store. Though her aunt and uncle wanted her to consider college, Mattie was not interested. She was ready to break free and get a place of her own. After working about a year at the fabric store and part time in the evenings cleaning homes, Mattie had enough money to move out. Lela was totally against the idea but Johnny said Mattie had to learn how to care for herself.

The next three years were peaceful. Mattie worked, went out with friends, dated a few guys, and lived as she pleased in her tiny boarding quarters about four blocks from Lela and Johnny. During the fourth year life changed. Mattie had gained her new found independence but tragedy struck suddenly. One day, Pa Whiting and Matthew were chopping wood in the field and Pa Whiting just stop and dropped dead. Dr. Williams said he had a heart attack. Many people believed he died of a broken heart. Pa Whiting was buried alongside Ma Whiting under the great big oak tree. This was the first time Mattie had gone to the field since the death of her mother. Everything was just as she remembered. Even the rocking chair her mother died in was still in the same place on the porch. Mattie shed one last tear and left the field. Matthew continued to live on the land.

Matthew worked the land he loved so much. He fed the cattle, sold meat to the butcher and worked in the mines to support himself. Matthew lived a very simple life. His stuttered speech remained as a reminder the day the lightning storm hit him but otherwise he was normal. Matthew liked a few girls but none were interested in him since Matthew was a man of simple living. It seemed like most girls he liked wanted to live in the city and Matthew knew he was not suited for that kind of life. Matthew wanted a girl who wanted to live with him in his home where he had become a man.

During this year Mattie's eye caught sight of a particular minister in the Wednesday night reservation's bible study. Every Wednesday night most of the reservationists would meet in the town square under a tent and have bible study. At the time, the reservation bible study was either lead by Minister Lee or Minister Smith and for one hour they sang songs, read scripture and prayed prayers. Sometimes a minister passing through would come to lead the services. Now, this particular minister had come to the city to bury his aunt and to sell her home. In the city he heard from the Negroes about the reservation's lightning storms. He decided to take a visit and travel one day to the reservation. It was here Minister Eli Wright saw the lush land and tall trees and he decided he would make this his home. He bought a small lot and within the year had built him a fine home. He decided to keep his aunt's home in the city and rent it to borders. Many people thought Minister Wright was white with his fair skin and hazel green eyes. Mattie had never seen a more refined and distinguished man. His voice was commanding and strong. His stature was upright as he walked with a long stride. After the bible study lesson one evening, she was so entranced she did not realize she dropped her mother's lace handkerchief. Mattie returned to her sitting area under the tent and there was her most prize possession in the world.

As she picked up her handkerchief from her seat, a voice said, "Did you like the sermon tonight, mam?"

As she turned her head there he was, a tall, built and fair-skinned man with the whitest teeth she had ever seen.

"Oh yes, I enjoyed it very much." She returned the reply with a smile.

She did not know of his age but it appeared he must have been at least ten years older. As she went to say something she thought gazing in his eyes, He must think me a fool.

"Mam, will you?" he said.

"Will I what?" Mattie replied.

"Will you be coming back to hear me more often?"

"Oh yes. You'll see me again".

Mattie walked away with a brisk and happy demeanor. All that night she thought of his smile. The next few weeks Mattie made sure to get a good seat as she made it to bible study early. Lela and Johnny were proud to see Mattie be so diligent in her religious study. They did not know that some evenings Mattie would stay a few minutes longer to speak to Minister Wright. Their talks became long and she began to learn a lot about him. The two became friends and even a little more.

After many conversations Mattie learned Minister Wright lived up north in Chicago when his aunt died. Mattie could not imagine leaving a big city like Chicago but he assured her Chicago was not spectacular. He told her his father was Black and Spaniard and his mother was French Canadian. Minister Wright spoke of how he truly believed his father loved his mother. His mother had died during childbirth. His father finally remarried and he went on to have other siblings but often his stepmother casually looked over him because he was so fair skinned. Minister Wright left home, went on to seminary, and learned the trade of blacksmith. He finally fell in love with a woman named Sicily but after a year of marriage, she died of scarlet fever. He had no children. He had never seen a town like the reservation. This was the most beautiful and peaceful land he had ever seen despite the treacherous lightning storms. Mattie told him about the lightning storm that took her mother and how she saw her die.

One night while Minister Wright was walking her home, Mattie mentioned how her water pump was leaking. She had called the repair person but he was out of town for the week. Minister Wright decided to look at the water pump himself. They entered into her quaint flat. Minister Wright knew Mattie lived a simple life. Everything was clean and in its place.

As Minister Wright noticed the kitchen's water pump leaking he asked "Mattie do you have some tools?"

"Yes, Uncle Johnny left some tools here the last time he came." she replied. "Thank you so much for coming. I can't keep bothering my Uncle to always fix everything for me. "

Minister Wright took the wrench, took off his jacket, rolled up his sleeves and began to disassemble the water pump. Mattie looked on, amazed by his brilliant yet gentle hands.

"That should do it." Minister Wright said.

"Thank you" Mattie said.

Minister Wright gave the tools back. Mattie gently placed her body against his chest. His smell was intoxicating, his shirt was soft and before Minister Wright knew it he dropped the tools to the floor and had begun to hold Mattie passionately in his arms. He had not felt the softness of a woman in years. Mattie surrendered to his soft tender lips. Her hands began to unbutton his shirt. Then Eli took her right arm and pressed her hand against his lips. He then buried his lips in her neck and smelled her sensuality. His hands had now made way to the back of Mattie's dress which he unbuttoned. The dress fell to the ground, Mattie's hands had made it to his belt and she unzipped his pants. They were exposed and free to love. Mattie's hands kept running over his chiseled chest. Eli's lips kissed her soft skin on her shoulders and at the top of her bust. Eli then carried Mattie into her room and placed her on the bed. He rose up for just a brief moment to look at her. He fell to the side of Mattie kissing her again. Eli then stopped, sat up, and lay on top of Mattie as he took both of his hands and held her face. It was that moment their embrace became a night of passion.

The next morning Minister Wright arose. He looked onto Mattie's delicate face and knew he had made a mistake. He quietly arose from the bed and put on his clothes. When he began to leave, he looked backed at Mattie sleeping peacefully. He went to leave when he saw paper and pen on her small desk in the living quarters. Minister Wright walked over to the small desk and wrote these words

"My darling, last night was beautiful but a mistake. I hope we will always be friends and I will always have a place for you in my heart, but this cannot continue for reasons I can't explain."

An hour later, Mattie awakened with a smile. She looked for Minister Wright but he had left. She was saddened he did not tell her good bye but she thought she would see him at the next bible study lesson. She turned to enter into the kitchen and admire the repaired kitchen water pump. Then she turned back and looked at the paper and pen on her desk in the living quarters. She walked over to notice the paper and pen were not as she had left it. She slowly picked up Minister Wright's note and read it with tears streaming from her eyes. She was hurt, embarrassed, and for the first time since her mother's death she felt completely and utterly alone.

Two months had passed since Mattie had seen Minister Wright. Since his desertion and recent marriage to Abigail Winters, Mattie had not gone back to the bible study lessons. She told everyone she had a job in the city on Wednesday evenings and Sundays cooking for an elderly white woman. Sunday the family still had dinner together. Matthew was just pulling up in the wagon. "I hear the sound of Matthew's horses. Mattie set the table please," Lela said.

Mattie had just come back from the city and was setting the table when her vision became blurred and suddenly she fainted with Matthew coming in the kitchen just in time to catch her. When Mattie awakened, she saw the face of Dr. Williams.
"She seems fine to me." Dr. Williams said as he placed his stethoscope in his bag. "Mattie, have you had these symptoms of fainting at any other time?"
"No sir."
Mattie remembered she had been feeling nauseated. Then she thought "Oh my God, it can't be."
"No Dr. Williams, I know what it is. I have been working longer hours." Mattie said.
"Well Mattie, today you need your rest. No more overdoing it."

"Yes Sir."

Uncle said, "Mattie, why you did not come to us for any money you needed? We would have given it to you."

"Uncle, you and aunt have done so much for me already. I am fine."

As Lela listened, she raised her left eye in curiosity and just smiled at Mattie. "Oh, Mattie" she thought.

Saturday as Mattie was preparing her breakfast of eggs, she could not cook bacon as the smell made her sick. She heard a knock at her door. She walked slowly to the door and looked through the peephole to see Lela standing on the other side of the door. For Lela to come by unannounced was strange. As she opened the door, Lela walked in the flat. She had come to check in on Mattie and make sure she was fine since last Sunday's spell.

"Oh Mattie, I see you're cooking breakfast." Lela said walking to the wooden oven.

"Yes, I am."

"Just eggs, no bacon Mattie?" Lela asked suspiciously.

"No, I ran out and forgot to go to the grocer."

As Lela looked around in Mattie's freezer, she said, "Why Mattie, here is bacon in your freezer. I will cook it for you."

"No Mam, That's ok."

"Mattie, just finish dressing or something and I will cook the bacon for you. Besides we have not talked in a while."

"Yes mam." Mattie said with a low tone.

As Mattie went to her room, she began to smell the bacon cooking and became nauseated. Suddenly, Mattie took a bag and began to regurgitate in a brown paper sack bag. Lela heard Mattie and immediately took the frying pan off the oven and ran in the room.

 "Mattie, are you sick?"

"The smell of the bacon is making me sick." Mattie replied.

"But Mattie you love bacon. It has never made you sick before. Maybe I should call Dr. Williams."

"Dr. Williams will not have a cure for this." Mattie said with a quaint smile.

Lela walked and stooped gently over and whispered into Mattie's left ear and said, "So when were you going to tell me about the baby?" All of Mattie's bronze color left her skin and Mattie became emotionless.

Chapter 5

Teardrops

Mattie's pregnancy was horrific. She had morning sickness day and night. Her aunt and uncle wanted her to move back home but she refused. Mattie told them the father was a guy she met while working in the city. Dr. Williams thought it best Mattie continue to work but only at the fabric store to occupy some of her time at home. He was extremely concerned about her emotional well-being. An arrangement with Mrs. Todd, the owner of the fabric store and Lela was agreed upon. Mattie would work as a seamstress from her flat. On Mondays, Lela would pick up the orders from the fabric store and take all the materials to Mattie and on Fridays Lela would bring the garments back. Mrs. Todd was able to oblige since her and Lela were close friends. Mattie was alone since most of the girls her age were now married and had moved. She grew more sadden by the day. She decided not to tell Eli since he had moved on with his life.

Over the next few months Lela was concerned about Mattie. Lela walked on eggshells around Mattie trying to determine what the real matter on Mattie's mind was. Mattie's appetite was almost non-existent. She would cry for hours at a time and did not seem to rest well. Dr. Williams told Lela this pregnancy was his most difficult case.

One Friday evening Lela had come to get the finished dresses she said to Mattie, "Mattie, your uncle and I was talking. We think it would be best if we helped you raised your child."

"Why do you think so?" Mattie asked.

"For the past few months you have been sickly and you seemed depressed."

"It is hard to be pregnant and alone."

"Maybe after the pregnancy we could take the baby for a little while, just until you get your faculties."

"Ok." Mattie replied in tears.

The day the baby came Lela was relieved. It was a long and slow labor that lasted for thirty three hours. It was during a lightning storm the child arrived. The thunders roared, the lightning kept the heavens lit, the rain poured and finally the baby screamed.

"Mattie, it's a girl!" Dr. Williams said. "You did it. "

Dr. Williams took the baby, cleaned and examined her. Afterwards, he swaddled her and gave her to Mattie.

"Hello, my little one. " Mattie said.

"She has all ten fingers and ten toes." Dr. Williams commented.

As Lela stood and looked she said, "Mattie she is beautiful."

"She is. I am going to name her Eve." Mattie smiled.

"She is beautiful. Johnny go get Satchel for the blessing. Eve has arrived." Lela said.

Within the hour Johnny arrived back home with Satchel. Satchel performed the usual blessing ceremonial ritual as Mattie, Lela, and Johnny watched in silence. Eve seemed to be at peace during the entire ritual and even made cooing noises. Satchel looked in the baby's eyes and spoke the word "Songbird". Lela thought this was a nice sweet name.

As Satchel ended the ritual he became perplexed. Though he made no mention to anyone else in the room he knew he had seen those eyes before. He could not remember if it was the eyes of a former ancestor, a run-a-way slave, or where he had seen those eyes before. He just knew these eyes were familiar. When Satchel left that evening he walked home with a lot on his mind.

"Hello my love! Ready for supper?" Dahlia asked when Satchel walked through the door.

"Yes, I am starved." Satchel replied as he entered the dining quarters and sat at the table.

"Is the baby healthy?" Dahlia asked.

"The baby is healthy and beautiful. Her name is "Songbird"

"Oh, Satchel, how sweet a name." Dahlia said with excitement.

"Yes, it is" Satchel answered in distress.

"What's the matter?"

"I don't know what it is but the child's eyes seem familiar to me. I have seen those eyes, but I can't remember just exactly where. Your Satchel is getting old. I use to have the memory of an elephant."

"My Satchel is not that old. I am sure you will figure it out. Well, let me get supper on the table." Dahlia said kissing Satchel on the cheek.

For the next two years Mattie was rarely seen on the reservation. She continued to work from home and went to church in the city on Sundays. She did not want Eli to become aware of Eve's existence as his daughter. It seemed that all the reservationists believed the story of poor Mattie falling in love with a traveling salesman who had abandoned her. Just as Mattie was about to relax on the couch to play with Eve the doorbell ranged. She thought what Aunt Lela wanted this day. She opened the door and there was Abigail Wright. Mattie was startled.

"Hello, Mattie Whiting." Mattie said while holding Eve in her arms.

"Yes, I am Mattie Whiting." Mattie said standing in awe.

"I am sorry to bother you Mattie, but it seems as if Mrs. Todd has sent my dress over to you for alterations and I was wondering if you had completed the alterations. I know it is not Friday, but tonight is my husband's and I anniversary and I wanted to wear the dress he loves so much. It is the blue dress with the sleeves trimmed in rose lace."

Mattie still standing in awe could not believe who was at her door.

 "The dress is ready. Come in and I will get it for you." Mattie responded putting Eve down.

Abigail walked in and spoke as Mattie hurried to get the dress from her bedroom while Eve followed swiftly behind but stop short of the bedroom door.

"You have a nice place here Mattie." Just as Abigail spoke Eve turned back to look at Abigail and Abigail looked at Eve with a startled response.

"Here is the dress." Mattie said while coming out of her bedroom.

"Yes, well thank you so much. You have a beautiful little girl." Abigail said.

"Thank you." Mattie responded.

"I better get going. Eli is waiting at home for me." Abigail said.

When Abigail left Mattie picked up Eve in her arms and hugged her tightly and said "She may think she has him, but I have so much more of him than she could ever imagine." Mattie said smiling at Eve.

Abigail rushed home in her wagon and all the time thinking how on earth could Eli have done this to her. When Abigail arrived home she hurried in to see Eli sitting on the couch waiting for her.

"I hope you are going to be ready soon. We have reservations at the best restaurant in the city and we need to be leaving." Eli said smiling at Abigail.

"I just need to put on my dress. I had to go to Mattie Whiting's flat to pick it up. Thank God she had it ready early." Abigail said while going to the bedroom to change clothes.

At that moment Eli thoughts drifted back to a time when he and Mattie walked home. He had missed her dearly but heard she had moved on. Meanwhile while changing into her dress it took all Abigail had to hold back the tears. Abigail looked at herself in the mirror and picked up her handbag and came out of the room running into Eli's arms. It was at this moment she decided to confront Eli.

"I love that dress. You look gorgeous tonight Mrs. Wright." Eli said.

"Thank you. Mattie did a fine job. I saw her baby tonight. She is a beautiful dark skinned bright eyed child." Abigail said while waiting for Eli's response that the baby was indeed of fair complexion.

"She is. I know Lela and Johnny are glad to have a little one in the family." Eli smiling while him and Abigail walked outside."

Abigail then thought Eli made no remarks of the child having fair skinned. He must have never seen the child. That means he doesn't know Eve is his child.

Abigail turned to Eli and said, "You know I love you and if there is ever anything you would like to talk to me about, you can. I love you too baby." Eli said with no unusual reaction. It was at that moment Abigail was certain Eli knew nothing of him being the father to Mattie's baby.

It was a month later after Abigail made the discovery that Satchel would discover the secret about Songbird's father. One day while Satchel made his usual Saturday walk through the reservation he heard a voice yell for him.

"Hello, Satchel." Eli spoke. "Can I see you for a moment. " Eli continued as he approached Satchel.

It was that moment Satchel looked like he had seen a ghost.

"What's the matter Satchel? You look like you have seen a ghost.

""No, Eli. It is just you and I don't speak much with your pastoral duties and well I never notice the mystic of your eyes."

"Thank you, I suppose." Eli replied.

"How can I help you?"

"Satchel, I need to speak with you about an important matter."

"Of course, you can speak to me about anything."

"It seems I went to see Doc Williams last week and I may have a stomach growth."

"What are you saying Pastor Wright?"

"I am saying it is possible I may not have long to live. I wanted you and the elders to know."

"What about your wife, Abigail?"

"I want to wait to tell her. I need to see how my condition will progress."

"Eli I have no words for you except I am sorry. "

"Don't worry about me Satchel. You and these people have been good to me. This land has been one of love and wonder."

67

"Well, we and the elders of course will do anything for you and Abigail."

"Thank you." Eli said. "I better get going it is almost time for lunch. Do you want to come with me Satchel?"

"No, actually I am going by to see songbird. That is Mattie's baby." Satchel said waiting for a startled reply.

"Yes, my wife told me she had seen Mattie's baby about a month ago."

"She did." Satchel responded in awe.

"Yes, she said the baby was beautiful."

"You should see the baby Eli. I believe she would be the most beautiful child you will ever know. "

"Thank you so much Satchel. I will do that soon. In the meantime I better be getting in for lunch."

"See you later, Eli." Satchel spoke.

"See you later Satchel." Eli replied.

Satchel walked away and he knew trouble was a brewing.

Sometime passed and Lela thought Mattie would feel better after Eve's birth, but Mattie appeared to be sad all the time. Eve grew to be a precocious child with daring adventures. Eve grew with a slightly noticeable right drop eyelid, but Dr. Williams assured Aunt Lela and Eve that the child was healthy.

One weekend Mattie decided to take Eve, now two and half years old, for a ride on the ponies at Mr. Palmerdale's pony farm and afterwards her and Eve would go by the pond and play with the turtle that had been there since Uncle Johnny could have remembered. Mattie and Eve walked about ten blocks. Eve loved to visit the ponies.

"Good morning, Mr. Palmerdale."

"Good morning, Mattie. You and Eve want to ride one of my ponies again"

"Yes, well pick a pony to ride. I am going back inside my house." Mr. Palmerdale said.

"Thank you Mr. Palmerdale."

"Look mama." Eve said pointing to one of the ponies.

"Yes, my dear."

Mattie picked up Eve and placed her on a pony. Mattie walked along side Eve and the pony. Her mind wondered to the day she lost her mother. She remembered how her and her mother would take long walks picking field flowers for the kitchen table. Suddenly, Eve fell to the ground. Mattie was startled as she ran to Eve on the other side of the pony. Eve seemed fine and there were no bruises. Mattie held Eve so close she nearly suffocated her.

"Sweetie, are you ok?"

"No mama, dirt hit head." Eve said pointing to her head.

"Oh, let me kiss it." With a kiss, Mattie said, "Is that better?"

"Yes, mama."

That evening Mattie walked Eve to her aunt's home. She could not imagine her life without Eve and yet she did not think she had enough love to give her. A few days later in the kitchen, Eve was at the kitchen table waiting on Lela to give her the left over cake batter. As Lela place the bowl on the table, Eve began to shake profusely, her eyes rolled back in her head, and she fell to the floor. Lela dropped the cake bowl and immediately fell to the ground beside her. As Johnny came in the kitchen to ask about dinner, Lela yelled "Get the Doctor, quick!" Johnny ran so fast out of the house he did not remember nothing but seeing Dr. Williams sitting on his porch and saying its Eve.

Doctor Williams went inside his house to get his bag and the two men ran as fast as they could. When they arrived Eve was still on the kitchen floor asleep.

"What happened?" Dr. Williams asked.

"I don't know, I was about to give her some cake batter and her eyes rolled back in her head, she shook to the ground, and . . ." as Lela cried.

"Has this happened before Lela?" Dr. Williams asked.

"Never!"

After several minutes, Eve awakened. Dr. Williams examined her and asked her a few questions like what was her name. She seemed to be fine but said she was sleepy.

Johnny took Eve to her room and laid her in the bed.

As they all stood over the child, Doctor Williams gave some instructions on what to do the next time this may happen.

"What are you saying Dr. Williams?" Lela asked.

"Eve has seizures. It may have been something that happened in child birth. Mattie was sick the entire pregnancy. The child may grow out of them but most likely she will have them all her life."

Lela and Johnny looked at Dr. Williams with great concern.

"Now don't worry I will give you a prescription to help the child sleep well at night."

"What if they continue like this all the time?" Johnny asked.

"Let's just trust God that they won't." Dr. Williams said patting Johnny on his shoulder.

The next day when Mattie came to see Eve, Lela told her what had happened. Mattie was surprisingly shocked. Lela said that Eve tried to tell them something later that day about her hitting her head but it didn't make any sense. She asked Mattie did she know anything. She decided it was best to keep the fall a secret. Mattie said what she could not imagine she could be speaking of.

"Mattie stay with Eve, I need to go to the druggist and pick up Eve's medicine. Watch her closely."

"Yes Mam."

Lela went to the druggist hurrying as fast as her legs could walk. The pharmacist said he would have the prescription ready by five o'clock. Hurrying to the druggist she tripped over a small stump in the pavement and oddly enough bumped into a man. She recognized him from the Wednesday bible study.

"Oh, I am sorry Minister Wright. Please forgive me."

"That's ok Mam, just slow down and be careful." He said looking into her eyes.

Lela looked at him with shocked.

"Mam are you ok?"

"Oh, oh yes."

"Be careful Mrs. Wyman."

"Yes sir" Lela said walking briskly. God had shown Lela just as plain as day as if He himself had come from the heavens. Minister Wright had a slightly drop right eyelid like Eve's. Oddly enough he seemed thinner than she had remembered. She had seen him but always at a distance in the pulpit, never close-up.

"Oh My God ", Lela thought in amazement.

That evening Lela returned with the medicine and Mattie went back to her flat and cried. She knew God did not want her to be a mother or wife. Look what she had done to her own child. Mattie was angry and she blamed herself for Eve's seizures. Maybe God was punishing her for still loving Eli.

Lela wanted to talk with her about Minister Wright but today did not seem like the right time. With Eve having seizures and Mattie acting so distant she did not know what to expect. She did not want her to run off with Eve nor did she want her to go away. Nevertheless, Lela would have to get to the bottom of this matter.

For the next few weeks Eve had a seizure about once a week and over the next few months the seizures began to become fewer and far between. Lela wanted Mattie to spend more time with Eve but thought maybe the child's illness was too much for her emotionally. Lela remembered Mattie before Ma Whiting passed. Mattie was happy and carefree but after the lightning storm she was never the same. Lela prayed and prayed that Mattie would stop believing that somehow she must have been the blame for her mother's death. Lela explained to her as a child that "Life Happens" and God has control. But in Lela's heart she knew it would mean nothing until Mattie came to know God for herself and that this is "God's world and His way".

This Saturday morning Lela decided to go to Mattie's flat unannounced. When she heard the early doorbell Mattie knew who it was. She thought Aunt must have pieced together the cause of Eve's seizures. As Mattie opened the door there Lela stood with a stern look.

"Yes mam." Mattie spoke softly.

"Mattie, we need to talk."

"Aunt it was an accident."

"I would say, and a big accident Missy." Lela said with a commanding tone.

"I didn't mean it."

"Oh really, he is a married man." Lela said as Mattie simultaneously spoke "I was walking alongside Eve and she fell off . . ."

"What did you say?" they both asked in unison.

"I know Minister Wright is Eve's father. What about Eve falling?" Lela asked with great concern.

Mattie now in tears said "She fell off one of Mr. Palmerdale's ponies and hit her head. There was no bruise or bump. I thought she was fine. As far as Minister Wright is concerned, I became pregnant two months before his marriage. I decided best not to tell him."

"And so he does not know about Eve." Lela gasped.

"No Mam, he doesn't know. That is why I began to take Eve to church with me to the city on Sundays. I did not want him to know."

"No wonder you have been so sad child. All this weight you carrying. You are going to have to let it go, Mattie. "

Lela left Mattie sitting on the couch emotionless as she stood up with a glance at Mattie. She turned slowly and walked out of the flat. Lela suddenly became tired walking home slowly. She had to think what was best for Eve. Lela came in the house to find Johnny and Eve sitting on the screened porch in the rocking chair. Johnny looked at Lela crying. Essie and Johnny Jr. were in the back room studying their parts for a church play.

"What's wrong baby?" Johnny asked as Eve was sleep in his lap.

"I am tired Johnny, I am tired." Lela said walking slowly inside the house.

That evening when everyone was sleeping peacefully Lela told Johnny about Minister Wright being Eve's father and Eve falling off Mr. Palmerdale's ponies and hitting her head on the ground. While Lela spoke Johnny looked worried and distressed. "Johnny, what is it now? I cannot take much more. I can see on your face there is something you are not telling me." Lela responded with dismay.

"No my love, everything is fine. I will handle things. You just rest." Uncle Johnny decided to see Minister Wright the next day. After work he made a stop by Minister's Wright home.

"Hello Johnny." Minister Wright said as Johnny walked up his steps.

"Hello."

"Minister Wright can I see you for a moment and alone."

"Of course. Let's take a walk to my back yard and see my wife's new tomato tree." Minister Wright groaned.

"Are you ok Eli?"

"No Johnny. My condition is getting worse. I probably don't have long. I want to thank you and all the elders for keeping my illness a secret. This stomach growth is getting larger every day. I had to go ahead and tell my wife. I could not hide the pain any longer."

"That is why I am here. There is something you need to know. I know about you and Mattie."

Eli stopped as he looked at Johnny.

"Eli, Mattie's child is your child." Johnny continued.

"I knew of a child but the people said the child's father was a traveling salesman or something."

"Mattie lied to us. The child has your right drooped eyelid and fair skinned."

It was at that moment Minister Wright knew Eve was his child as Johnny handed him a picture of her.

"She looks exactly like me when I was a child. That explains that strange conversation I had with Satchel a few months ago. We were talking of the new fruit trees on my property and just out of the clear blue he told me Mattie's child was one of the most beautiful children he had ever seen. He said it would be of great interest to see the child and that even I would not be able to deny the child's beauty. I think Satchel may have figured it out, not unless Mattie told him." Eli mentioned.

"No, I know Mattie well. She didn't tell Satchel anything. Satchel has a way of knowing things about you that no one else knows, including you sometimes. One thing we know about Satchel, he won't say a word to anyone." Johnny responded

"Johnny come inside the house. I am going to give you something and please keep this between us."

"Of course Eli. You know you can trust me."

As the two men walked alongside the front of the home Johnny had to assist Minister Wright as his stomach pain had suddenly become unbearable. Minister Wright began to think to himself how he hurt Mattie and maybe this stomach growth was God's punishment. Though he loved his wife Abigail, his motives for marrying her were for selfish reasons. He felt pressured to marry and to have children with a woman more of his age. Always trying to please others had caused him misery. He knew from the first time he saw Mattie he loved her. He was able to confide in her about the loss of his first wife and the pain he had carried for so many years. He thought how could he have betrayed Mattie? How could he have hurt Mattie and Eve? His heart was toiled with agony. He had thought these last few years he had done what was right but he forgot "A man's way is right in his eyes, but the Lord pondereth the heart." He was in great distress. He thought Mattie had moved on by now. She disappeared it seemed. He heard she had a child as his wife Abigail said she saw Mattie with a beautiful dark colored child. He just shrugged it off. The thought of it all was too much for him to bear. Johnny could see the concerned look on Minister Wright face.

"Eli" Johnny said," Do not worry. I thought you should know that you have a child. Most people do not say anything about Mattie because they know what happened to her mother when she was a child. She has been strange ever since. In fact, she never speaks or asks anything about her mother."

As Minister Wright heard Uncle Johnny, he could not think of such a thing, as Mattie was sweet to him.

"But Johnny, Mattie has always spoken of her mother to me. She told me how her mother and she would take long walks in the fields. She even spoke of the day when she saw her mother die."

Uncle Johnny replied with shock, "She saw it! She never said a word to any of us."

"Yes, she saw the lightning strike."

The two men made their way inside the house. Minister Wright took Uncle Johnny to his office where he closed the door. Minister Wright, with the help of Uncle Johnny walked to his desk and chair and wrote two bank notes to be given to John Banks.

"Johnny take these two paper notes to Mr. Banks. This should help." Eli said in pain.

Johnny looked at the bank notes and said, "Eli how you come to have this money?"

My mother was French Canadian and she and my aunt came from a wealthy family. Tomorrow I will see Mims and work out something else. "

"Eli thank you."

"No Johnny, thank you. At least now I know I won't leave this earth without a little part of me still remaining. I would like to see the child soon."

"I will see what I can do." Johnny said.

Now Johnny had two paper notes of one thousand dollars each for Mattie and Eve. He would see Eli within the week to discuss the other provisions.

Johnny went home to Lela and told her he had taken care of everything. He also told her Mattie had witnessed the lightning strike that killed her mother. Lela could not think how Mattie could have held such a secret.

Now as soon as Johnny left, Eli made his way to Eve's apartment. It took all his strength to get his wagon and horse and make his way to see her. As he knocked on the door, it opened as Mattie was leaving to take Eve to Lela.

"Minister Wright" Mattie said shockingly holding Eve.

"Mattie, I need to speak with you," Minister Wright said waking in.

"Why did you not tell me about the child? " Minister Wright said looking at Mattie and Eve.

"About Eve", Mattie said sharply, "For what, you're married. You made a fool of me." She yelled back to him. "Go away. Go away." Mattie continued to yell as Eve cried.

As Mattie began to cry and Eli could see her tears of pain and agony. As he walked slowly and in pain towards Mattie, he touched and smelled her and Eve's hair and he whispered in Mattie's ear "No matter what, I will always love you." He kissed Eve on the forehead and he left.

The next day word rang throughout the reservation that Minister Wright had died early that morning in his sleep. Johnny was glad he had talked to Minister Wright when he did. In the meantime, Johnny set up an account for Eve and Mattie. He never told Mattie Eli knew Eve was his child or about the money and Mattie never told him or Lela of Eli coming to see her and Eve the night before his death. Mattie was saddened when she heard the news and could not forgive herself of the last words she spoke to Minister Wright. She was heartbroken and blamed herself even for Eli's death.

Johnny and Lela decided to go to see Eli's body and that Mattie and Eve should be present. Lela would leave Essie and Johnny Jr. with Ms. Emma. As they hurried off and rushed inside Samuel's funeral home, no one was around. The four walked down the aisle to see the body. There Minister Eli Wright lay in a glass casket. His fair skinned gave light. He had on a black suit with a gray shirt and a vibrant rose pink striped tie with the matching handkerchief. His black shoes were the shiniest Eve had ever seen as they reflected light. His cufflinks and tiepin were of pure gold. His haircut nicely edged and in his right hand he held his Mahogany leather bound Bible. As they stood, no one notice how Eve had somehow climbed the glass casket to look at the body or that Satchel stood at the back of the chapel looking on. Johnny immediately picked Eve up and said they had better be going, as people should be arriving soon. As Lela nodded her head in agreement, she and Johnny turned to walk away. Nevertheless, Mattie stood to look at Eli once more and as she went to kiss his cheek a tear fell from her right eye and she said softly in his ear, "I will always love you." At that moment, Mattie fell to the birch hardwood floor and beside Eli's casket, she belted out with a scream "Oh God!" Johnny went to give Eve to Lela but she refused.

Lela looked at Johnny and said "Let her cry, Let her cry it all out." Moreover, suddenly a thunder roared as a lighting storm was coming near.

Mattie screamed repeatedly, "Oh God, Oh God!" After a few minutes, she stood up taking notice of the thunder outside the chapel and turned to walk away and there was Lela standing there with open arms. Walking away, they could see Abigail standing in the back of the aisle waiting to view her husband's body before the funeral services. Lela and Abigail gave each other blank stares. Lela nodded for Johnny to take Mattie and Eve outside to the wagon. Lela turned back to Abigail.

"Abigail, I am sorry about your loss." Lela said with compassion.

"I do not know what I am going to do."

"You knew all along didn't you Abigail."

Abigail looked with those big brown eyes and said, "Yes, when I went to get my dress from Mattie's flat I saw that child with my husband's eyes."

79

"Did you question him about it?"

"He never said anything to me so I kept quiet." Abigail said innocently.

"Abigail you were his wife. You never thought he did not say anything because he did not know."

"I never gave it much thought."

"A woman knows when her husband is keeping secrets. Intuition and suspicion is every woman's gift from God." Lela replied.

"I have been through so much Lela, especially since his illness and besides this is not the time."

As Abigail went to walk away, Lela grabbed her arm "You knew all along that he did not know about Eve and yet when your husband became ill you said nothing. You were going to let him die without knowing he had a child."

"Mattie is at fault as well. She said nothing to him of the child." Abigail replied.

"You knew Mattie was young and not well. May God have mercy on your soul." Lela said in a firm voice.

As Lela walked out to the wagon Johnny met his wife to help her on the wagon and Satchel seeing the events was glad the truth had finally been revealed and thought Mattie may finally have some peace.

"What's wrong Lela?"

"I will tell you later." Lela replied.

The next few months were peaceful. The rain storms had ceased for now and the weather was cool. One night while turning in for bed Lela asked "Johnny you got other children out there somewhere."

"Why hell no! Whatever gave you that idea?" Johnny replied.

"You know I have seen Abigail at a few of the bible studies. She just looks at me and turns her head and remains the devoted widow. This is Minister's Wright's only child to date. Children are God's way of smiling on the world."

"Now dear, let it go. Anyway, we are doing fine. Do not worry about Abigail. You know Lela it may be hard for her since she does not have children. Remember those years we had no children. I could see the sadness and pain in your eyes Lela Wyman. I prayed for God to do a miracle and he did more." After a pause Johnny continued and asked, "Baby if I may ask, how did you know Abigail knew of Eve?"

"God told me. Just like the night my sister died. I woke in a sweat and I knew I had lost my sister. Sometimes Johnny I can look at people and I see right through them."

Johnny looked and smiled at his wife and that night he and Lela fell asleep in each other's arms.

That same night Satchel took a short walk to the pond where he and turtle sat quietly. Satchel looked into the heavens and prayed, "Father God, show me continually how to help your children that they may live in peace."

Chapter 6

Leadership

The following Saturday while Satchel took his usual walk around the reservation Federal officers approached Satchel's front door and just as one went to knock on the door they heard a voice behind them, "May I help you?" Dubose asked hoping Dahlia would not come to the door.

The officers turned around to see Dubose. The tallest officer in the middle said," We are looking for the Indian Satchel."

"Why he is taking his walk around the reservation? I couldn't tell you when to expect him. "

"We are in no hurry. We will just wait." An officer replied.

"Well, I will stand outside and just wait with you." Dubose commented.

After about a twenty minute wait Satchel approached the officers.

"Hello Dubose." Satchel said.

"Hello Satchel." Dubose replied.

"So you are the great Satchel." The officer said.

"How can I help you?" Satchel asked.

"My name is Federal Patton. I am here to give you're the orders from the United States Federal Government and from my commanding officer Colonel Benjamin that you and these people must leave this land in thirty days. The government is planning to use this land to extend the railroad. The Federal government is willing to give you some compensation for this land."

"What if we don't want to leave?" Satchel casually asked.

"Well, we will move you." Officer Patton said while standing only a finger's length from Satchel's face.

"You can't do this. This is Satchel's land." Dubose shouted.

"Calm down Dubose, this gentleman is just doing his job." Satchel replied while looking into Dubose's eyes.

Officer Patton then slapped the papers in Satchel's chest and him and his officers walked away.

"Why, Satchel what are we going to do?" Dubose asked.

"First of all Dubose the government is not planning to extend the railroad through this awful part of the land. No, I have a feeling Officer Patton is looking for something."

"What could that be?"

"Gold" Satchel smiled.

"Satchel, you have never mentioned gold on this land. Is there gold here?" Dubose asked with excitement.

"It depends. What do you consider gold?" Satchel smiled again.

The following day, Johnny, Lela, Essie, Johnny Jr., Matthew, Mattie and Eve were having supper when they heard a knock at the door. Johnny got up and walked to the door and there was Satchel.

"Hello Satchel, what brings you here?"

"Johnny tonight the men are gathering under the big tent at six pm. We have some important business to discuss."

"Well for you to come by the house means it's important! I will be there."

Johnny told Lela some of the men of the town were meeting tonight but nothing anyone should worry about.

That night as Johnny met with the others all the men of the reservation that could be there was there.

"What on earth?" Johnny thought.

"Men, today we have a proposition from the federal government. They are going to take the land." Satchel began.

The voices in the audience went in an uproar.

"Order, order! We don't have a choice in the matter. They will pay us something." Satchel said.

"You mean they are going to pay you something. This land is actually yours Satchel." Someone spoke.

"You do not think I would not take the money for myself. You all are my people and my responsibility." Satchel proudly spoke.

"You mean we have to tell our wives and children we have to move."

"Yes." Satchel replied.

"They are giving us one month for this land to be cleared and they are going to burn it down whether we leave or stay. I have known most of you men from the day you came to the reservation and I am going to miss you all. Nothing we can do." Satchel spoke.

"They want the land Satchel? Why now?" a voice in the crowd asked.

"Haven't you heard? Rumor for years has been we have gold hidden on this land." Someone replied.

"Men I did not argue with them. Let them take the land. But we must leave. I don't want any fighting or death. Believe me when I say it just isn't worth it. Go home and tell your families to pack. "Satchel replied.

The men turned away to go tell their families. Johnny walked home noticing something was strange in the air and noticed the night clouds moving fiercely.

The next two days on the reservation the people were sad. People's faces were tearful. In three weeks the land would be bulldozed or burned and the government would only pay them only about one third of what their land was worth. Some of the people were going to go stay with other family members who lived in other parts of the country, some would move to other squalors where only blacks stayed and a few decided to die with the land. But the people decided with everything they had all been through they were family and maybe if they could find other land they would stay together. In the meantime Satchel signed the papers and he calculated the amount of money each family would receive.

It was Wednesday night and the bible study had to be canceled. The worst storm was approaching the reservation. Dubose had gone over to Satchel's home and needed to talk to him about some important matters when the thunderous voice of God was more powerful than any of the some of the oldest people on the reservation had ever heard. Satchel and Dubose would have to put their conversation on hold. Both men made their way to the church and Satchel rang the church bell for the first time ever. The people knew this meant to come to the church. People were coming as fast as they could with their most precious belongings. At the church Satchel and the elders holding open an underground door that the people were to enter. Ted Mims Esquire and Timothy Cook were passing out candles to the adults. Some knew of the land's underground cave and some thought it was a rumor. All now two hundred and six persons entered that door and Satchel was the last person in the tunnel.

"Please, listen everyone." Satchel spoke holding a candle "I have been on this land since the beginning and I have never seen the wind so fierce. I believe it is best we stay here. We have enough room for us all."

"But Satchel it is just thunder and windy. It has not begun to rain yet." someone spoke from the crowd.

"I know, but something is different tonight. I think it is best. If nothing happens at least everyone now knows where the underground shelter is." Satchel replied.

"Satchel what is this place?" Someone asked.

"It was a tunnel for those who were slaves to run as they made their journey to freedom. For my ancestor it was a tunnel that my ancestors used as shelter from the storms."

The tunnel was the darkest of places even with candles and some people said they could smell the scent of death. The winds roared, trees fell, hail came, and the lightning lit the heavens. Emma spoke softly to Lela, "I don't know who done it but God is more than angry. "

"I agree, this is the worse I have ever seen." Lela replied.

The rage of God went on for thirty six hours. The people sat and prayed as they knew God was in an uproar about something. After two days in the underground shelter, Satchel, Ted Mims, Esquire, Minister Lee and Smith, Dr. Williams, Noah Carter, John Banks, Timothy Cook, Elder Dubose and Johnny went out and told the others to stay until they return. As the men slowly made their way to the door of the tunnel one by way they walked up the twenty steps and entered into the daylight of the reservation. What they saw was beyond the scope of God. Every building, every home, the school, even the church had been leveled. No tree stood and no bird sung. Dead animals of horses and cows could be seen. The men standing in a line side by side were silent for ten minutes when suddenly three horses came upon them. It looked like Uncle Jonny's, Satchel's, and Timothy's horses.

Then Satchel said, "We must have done something to anger Him. Everything is gone but these three horses." Just as Satchel finished speaking a cow came up from behind with a "moo".

"Excuse me Lord, and the cow." Satchel responded by lifting his heads to the heaven.

The men walked the area being careful of fallen debris. They could not begin to imagine how on earth they were going to tell the others and how to start putting the pieces of their lives together.

"Well men it may take a while but we are going to cash in the T-bills." said Elder Dubose.

"T-Bills" All the men sounded in amazement.

"That is what I wanted to talk to you about Satchel before the storm came. You see men, every month I take up the money from families for the reservation. I am responsible for the finances of the land.

"Yes but I thought the money was for the upkeep of the land." Minister Lee said.

"It is not only for the upkeep of the land but for the reservation people to have investments. I guess Mims you need to tell the others." Elder Dubose replied.

"I incorporated the reservation. For years now we have used a portion of the monies to invest in government T-Bills. Now it is a small investment." Mims said.

"I always thought the citizen dues were a little high." Noah Carter said scratching his head.

"How were you all able to do this?" Johnny asked. "You know that's white folks business."

"Look at me. In everyone's eyes I am a white." Timothy Cook said.

Timothy Cook could pass for a white man any time he wanted. He looked like the mayor's son. He was lily white with dark brown hair and blue eyes, his mother was European and his father was a fair skinned black man.

"About ten years ago Cook went up north to visit some family. During that visit, a banker approached him and told him about T-Bills. When Timothy told the agent he lived in a community and could probably get others to join in the deal was done. The banker told him how to go about it. When Timothy came back and told Mims and myself of the opportunity we incorporated the land and signed all the signatures. Paperwork was sent up north. We sent twenty five dollars a month to invest in government T-bills for the last ten years." Elder Dubose replied.

"Do you have those T-Bills?" Satchel said.

"Yes, every month I gave Banks the T-Bills." Mims replied.

"If it is those letters you gave me Mims then they are in the safe with the money." Banks answered. "I got the safe with me in the tunnel. One thing my daddy taught me and that is don't ever leave your money in the bank."

"Timothy we owe you." Satchel said.

"No you don't. The reservation was the only place that accepted me for who I was and I wanted to take care of it just like it had taken care of me." Timothy replied.

"Thank you Timothy. It looks like Timothy and Mims are going up north to handle some business. Men let us agree to only cash in seventy percent of the T-bills. Let's keep some in reserved just in case we have another storm." Satchel replied while all the men nodded in agreement.

"What are we going to tell the rest of the folk?" Noah Carter asked.

"For now we are going to have to live underground. We will tell them we are working on things and by the month end we will have a new land. We will deal with the government later. But for now Timothy you and Mims better go north and quick before the news of this disaster spreads." Satchel replied.

"Yes sir." Both Timothy Cook and Mims replied.

The men decided to take a horse in the city and catch a train for the rest of the travel. Surprisingly the city had little damage. It would probably be a few days before someone in the city came to the reservation and went back to report the devastation.

That night Timothy and Mims left. It was a week's journey by train. Timothy was able to convince the train manager Mims was with him and he needed his butler to sit close by. Timothy said he and the Negro had an important business matter. The train manager agreed although they would have sit on the last passenger sit in the back of the first class coach. Mims never thought he would ever ride first class but even to be in the back of first class for him was just fine. Fortunately, they arrived safely. When they arrived they immediately went to handle the business having barely slept during the entire trip. Mr. Daniels was excited to see Timothy coming in his bank. Mims stayed outside during the transaction.

"Why Mr. Cook, what can I do for you today?" Mr. Daniels asked.

"Everything is gone. I am here to cash in some of those T-bills." Timothy said as he tipped his hat.

"Why, what happened?"

"Had a great storm" Timothy said as he wanted to give Mr. Daniels as little details as possible.

"Why I will be happy to oblige. To get everything settle it will take about two days."

"Anyway you can make it sooner? The people have no money and are starving."

"Come back tomorrow. My assistant and I will work through the night. Be back tomorrow around three o'clock."

"Thank you sir." Timothy said shaking Mr. Daniels hand.

As Timothy came outside he tipped his hat ever so slightly and pointed up with three fingers to Mims who was standing across the road. Mims had to stay in the color hotel and Timothy stayed at the white hotel. Timothy got a room and immediately went upstairs. Not speaking to anyone and no one expecting a thing."

The next day Timothy stayed in his room all day. At three o'clock he promptly met the insurance agent. Mims could see him enter the office from across the road. At four o'clock he and Mims met at the train station. Both men were nervous as the last train left at five o'clock. Timothy bought tickets for the both of them as he explained to the foreman Mims was his personal butler. Both men did not speak as Mims made sure to stand behind Timothy at all times. They stepped on the train only to hear of a person speaking of a devastating storm on one of the Indian's reservations. During the entire trip neither man said nothing until they step off the train and was out of the city.

"That was dangerous." Timothy said.

"Very." Mims replied.

"Did he suspect anything Tim?"

"Nothing."

"'Did everything go ok?"

"Yes." Timothy replied.

"Do you think the banker will discover that you are black and lived on the reservation?" Mims asked.

"He already knows. The banker is my brother who has been passing since the day he was born. He got into banking about fifteen years ago." Timothy smiled.

"Timothy, I am glad you and your brother are white men." Mims said while both men laughed out loud. Meanwhile on their way back Satchel met with the federal government officers. They came a week before the people were too moved. Federal officers had come with money in hand and to see if they could get the people off the land sooner than the contract had specified. As Officer Patton appeared on horse, there stood Satchel waiting by himself.

"Look like you Niggers and Indians had a disaster. Once again it looks as if you are the last man left standing." Officer Patton said getting of his horse and laughing with the other officers.

"You see the smoke yonder, "Satchel said pointing to his left, "The others are there around the camp fire cooking dinner."

"Well I see you folks survived the storm after all."

"I thought you be coming today with the money. I see you have a small purse in your hand." Satchel replied.

"From the looks of things looks like I will just take this land off your hands and keep the money. The land isn't worth anything. " Officer Patton replied as he went to turn around.

"Before you turn around on horse, Officer Patton, I thought you may want to know we sent our lawyer Mims with the contract to see Colonel Benjamin who I believe you said is your Commanding Officer. We wanted to show him the contract he had signed."
Federal Patton stood and bit his lip.

"Oh, that's right." Satchel continued, "Colonel Benjamin knows nothing of the deal. You signed his name. If you don't give me the money right now Mims is going to miss my telegraph message. He is only one hour away from telling Colonel Benjamin about you and this land deal he knows nothing about. I guess you wanted to keep all the gold on this land you are expecting to find." Satchel said.
Officer Patton dropped the small purse of money on the ground and Satchel picked it up with caution. Satchel opened the purse and counted the money as Officer Patton looked on with bitterness.

"When Niggers and Indians learned to read, it changed the world. " Satchel said smiling.

"You and your Niggers better get off the property by the date on the contract." Officer Patton said getting back on his horse and leaving with his fellow officers.

The journey was stressful but Timothy and Mims had returned with the money. The reservation bought another land about twelve miles away that was for sale near Matthew's home. When Matthew came that Sunday and saw the reservation he knew his neighbors were leaving to live with their children up north. He told Satchel of the couples' desire to sell the land and within the next two weeks an agreement was made. The people were set and ready for their journey to the land. Strangely enough when Satchel left the tunnel he seemed to be carrying a covered box with holes.

"Satchel, you want me to help you with that." Johnny asked.

"No, I can manage." Satchel replied.

"Satchel, it looks so heavy. Besides, I don't remember you having that when we went underground." Johnny said.

"I am fine Johnny."

"Satchel, what are you hiding? It's not the turtle by the pond that the children play with? How did you get him?"

Satchel replied with only a smile.

Saying no more Johnny walked on ahead.

The others traveled on and Satchel stopped. When he could see them in a distance he turned around and looked at the ravaged land. He remembered his family, the death of his tribe and even the day he met "Yellow Moon". He kept thinking about how long he had lived on this land and all he had witnessed and endured. Then, Satchel went back inside the tunnel. Just as Satchel entered the tunnel and made his way to the last step beneath the door he bent over and moved the concrete step to the side. There he took his hands and put it in the hole that lay beneath and pulled out a leather satchel with strap. Five minutes has passed before Satchel came back out and he lit fire to the tunnel door. He turned forward, picked up his bag and placed the strapping around his neck and shoulder and held the covered box in his left hand as he got on his horse, and caught up with the others. After a ten minute walk the people heard several explosions in the distance. It scared them but

Satchel was not disturbed as he rode forward. The people looked at him and without question continued to move forward.

Chapter 7

Unity

After the most terrible month of their lives the two hundred and six people moved to their new land. For the next few years, the people worked the land and build again. Some of the men went to work in the coal mines with Matthew during the day. It did not matter where the people decided to build their homes, the land flourished. The green grass, the honeysuckle trees, vegetable gardens, white picket fences, and starry moons were becoming common. God's lightning storms still appeared on occasions but were more quiet and gentle in nature. Even the rains that fell were nothing more than fine mist. God's grace and mercy had sustained their life with a new land and hope. Oddly enough the old reservation was ravaged by officers looking for gold but none was ever discovered.

Johnny and Lela could not be happier and this was the year Essie had left again for the fall to go back to the black college in the city for her last year of matriculation. She would then return as a teacher for the new reservation school. Essie had grown to become a fine young lady.

Essie was not like the other college girls. She was quite shy and often stayed home in the dorms on Friday nights and read books. There was one particular Friday night that her roommate Claire Hughes asked Eve to come with her to one Negro city dances. Essie refused but Claire persuaded her to come along anyway. That evening getting dress Essie was nervous and petrified. During the dance all the men would ask a lady to dance and they danced in harmony as the music played. Essie just sat in a chair at one of the tables in back of the room watching Claire dance with

John Franks, one of seniors at the college. Essie thought they made a beautiful couple. While Essie sat she heard a voice asked, "Would you like to dance?"

Essie turned and looked upward to find a tall dark skinned fellow smiling at her. Though shy Essie stood and with her hand the two dance.

"What is your name, Mam?"

"My name is Essie Wyman. And what is your name sir?"

"I am Sebastian Knight."

It would be for the next several months the two were inseparable and Essie thought maybe this could be her husband. She loved Sebastian with all your heart since he had been the only man ever to show her interest. It would be on a Friday evening when Essie hurried to her room to change clothes to meet Sebastian for dinner that night. Her physics test took longer than expected and she hope Sebastian would not be worried about her being a little late. As she made her way off the campus two blocks over there was Sebastian waiting and he seemed furious.

"I am sorry I am late Sebastian, but my test took longer than expected. " Essie responded.

"Let's just get going. We are supposed to be meeting my boss and his wife tonight and here you are embarrassing me."

"Why I am sure they will understand, besides I am only twenty minutes late." Essie said while Sebastian and she walked briskly in the alley twenty feet from the restaurant entrance.

"Just twenty minutes." Sebastian said and then he struck her along her face. Essie stood holding her left cheek and in shocked.

Sebastian looked at Essie and with great sympathy apologized. "I am sorry. I never meant to hurt you my love. I must be under more stress than I realize." Sebastian said as Essie slowly step back two feet.

"Look baby, I have been stressed with work and trying to get this promotion so I can save money so we can get marry. Please forgive me baby. Please." Sebastian said.

Essie wanted to run away and go back to the campus but her love for Sebastian was greater so she stayed and that evening she and Sebastian had dinner with his boss and his wife.

Essie always returned home every weekend to spend time with the family but this last school term it seemed as if Essie was missing more and more weekends away from home. After missing one month of weekends Essie appeared one Saturday.

"I am glad to finally see my daughter." Lela said as Essie walked up the small steps.

"Oh Ma, I have been busy that is all." Essie replied.

"Aunt Essie" Eve said as she jumped into Essie's arms.

"My you are becoming a big girl."

As Eve went to hug Essie she said, "Did a big bee bite you?"

Lela stopped strangely and what she expected to see was even worse.

"Eve go inside, I need to speak with your Aunt Essie. "

Eve ran inside and Lela said, "What on earth is that mark across your neck?"

"It is nothing Ma. I just had an accident."

Lela grabbed Essie's arm asking, "Has someone been hitting on you?"

"Of course not Ma."

"Essie Wyman do not lie to me. What is going on up there at that school?"

"Nothing Ma, now please let me go."

Lela released Essie's arm and said nothing more about it. That evening the family had the usual supper and Essie seemed fine as she laughed with Johnny Jr. and Matthew. Johnny could tell something was bothering Lela but thought it best they talked about it later.

That night as Johnny and Lela went to turn in for bed Johnny asked, "Lela what is wrong?"

"Essie came home today with a mark on her neck."

Johnny laughed at first. "I thought you had that talk with Essie?"

"Not that kind of mark Johnny, but a bruise."

Johnny grew still and quiet and both he and Lela said no more.

The next Sunday evening as Essie went to return by railroad to the city, she got off the train platform and there was her Sebastian.

"Essie stop slobbering all over me." He said while she hugged him.

"I was just happy to see you."

"Let's go. What took you so long? "

"I had to go visit my family."

As Essie and Sebastian walked back to the campus as he grabbed her arm the entire way. They entered into the common area just before they stepped on campus and he said "You don't go anywhere again unless I tell you."

"Why, Sebastian I just went to the reservation to visit my family?" Essie said. As she spoke Sebastian hit her and Essie began to bleed from the mouth.

"You stupid woman. You think I don't know you have been seeing someone else. You come here." Sebastian pulled Essie by her hair and threw her to the ground. He went to hit Essie again but this time Essie took her legs and wrapped them around his legs and Sebastian came falling to the ground. Essie was screaming for help but it seemed no one could hear. She went to get up to run but Sebastian had grabbed her arm. As she went to pull away there was a clicking sound Sebastian's Ear.

There was Johnny standing over Sebastian with his loaded rifle. "You hit my daughter one more time and your mother will bury your body without your head."

Essie was startled as she quickly stood.

There from the bushes that surrounded the common area appeared with aimed rifles Johnny Jr., Matthew, Satchel, Timothy Cook, Minister Lee, Minister Smith, Ted Mims Esquire, Elder Dubose, John Banks and Noah Carter.

"Now if you decide to fight us all then your mother won't be able to even bury the body." Johnny continued to speak as then Dr. Williams came out from the far bush on the left. Johnny then said, "We bought our doctor along just in case it would have to come to that."

"You don't touch reservation people." Satchel said.

Sebastian got up extremely slow as Johnny's rifle stayed pointed at his head.

"What is your name and how did you meet my daughter? " Johnny asked. After a brief silence he then said. "You better speak or I will shoot." Johnny said.

"My name is Sebastian Knight and I work as a blacksmith in town. We met at a dance one night."

"How long you been dating?"

"Just this fall semester."

"Go find some other man's daughter to hit. Now Git." Johnny said waving his rifle. Sebastian ran as fast as he could and fortunately was never seen again.

Essie stood crying while Satchel held her tightly and said, "Now dear don't worry. You only have another semester and the elders and I are going to take turns and go to school with you this spring."

"Don't do that. "Essie sobbed.

"We have worked it all out. Besides I could use the vacation." Satchel said.

After Johnny explained the situation to the college campus president, from that day forward Satchel was able to get his long awaited formal education as he went to school with Essie for one semester. Satchel thought it was best he stay with Essie and travel with her back to the reservation on weekends. He was an old man and didn't need to work. At first Essie was ashamed to have the Indian walking around with her to class but she got to know Satchel much better and came to love him like a father. He even carried her books when he walked Essie to her classes.

Chapter 8

Friendship

Six years had passed and a lot had changed. Johnny Jr. began to work in the coal mines with Matthew and both married Satchel's granddaughters. Eve was a teenager now in the young adult class and had made friends with the twins Carolyn and Ann Cook. They were the daughters of Timothy Cook. The three girls became best friends and remained inseparable because other children would tease them calling the girls "passers". Carolyn and Ann always took care of Eve since they knew of her seizures. Once while walking home from school Eve fell to the ground with convulsions. Carolyn held her so that she would not hit her head and Ann went to get Dr. Williams and Lela. Sometimes Eve would have to rest for days at home and everyday Carolyn and Ann would stop by and catch Eve up on the day's lesson and the latest gossip. Surprisingly, the girls could sing. They had angelic voices, perfect harmony and pitch with no vocal training. The girls excited about their youthfulness could be heard after school singing and laughing while walking home.

One day Mrs. Jackson, a new reservation school teacher, was entering the classroom and she heard the three girls' melodic voices. "Where is this music coming from?" Ms. Jackson thought. Ms. Jackson was the second oldest child of the Cartwright family. She was a six feet and one inch in height. She was a shapely, curvaceous woman. She walked with excellent posture and stood as tall as the big oak trees on the new reservation. Her stature was one of confidence and her beauty was radiant with her brown eyes and maple honey skin. She spoke in a soft tone and she carried the name "Grace" with grace. The Cartwright families' were one of the wealthiest black families who had land in the city. She had married the love of her life Harold Jackson but after a few years he died of pneumonia. Her father, Nathaniel Cartwright was one of the very few men who had discovered gold in the mines during the early years of the emancipation. He grew his money in construction and he owned a mill in the city. It was his lumber who built Negro banks, schools, hospitals, and homes.

As Mrs. Jackson stopped before she entered the classroom the three girls abruptly stop singing.

"Girls don't stop! Go own. Continue."

The girls were nervous but continued singing.

"Ladies what are your names?"

"I am Carolyn."

"I am Ann."

"I am Eve."

Would you like to be in the chorus?

The girls were delighted to be offered an opportunity.

"Oh, Yes Mam" they all said in unison.

The principal Mr. Hughes told the girls they would have to wait to take chorus the following school term. They needed to fulfill certain curriculum requirements. But Ms. Jackson told Mr. Todd that was not acceptable and reminded him it was her father's lumber and money that helped built the new reservation school. Principal Todd somehow and someway changed the girls' curriculum requirement and Carolyn, Ann, and Eve, begin singing in the chorus.

Lela and Johnny was thrilled Eve was finding her way and her seizures had become less frequent. Not having any children, Ms. Jackson took a special likeness to Eve. Eve had a higher octave

range than Carolyn and Ann. It was one of the best voices she had
ever heard.   Mattie occasionally would come to here Eve sing at a
church or social event. Mattie now worked in the city as a maid for
the Mayor. Mattie felt a part of the Mayor's family more than she
did her own. The first time Mattie heard Eve sing solo she cried
thinking how proud Eli would have been. Of course, Johnny and
Lela were always there to support Eve. Oddly enough Mattie did not
like Ms. Jackson doting on Eve. She had become jealous of the
attention Eve was receiving from family and the others who lived on
the reservation. Ms. Jackson had quite a keen understanding of the
complexity of Eve's upbringing. She hired Eve to clean her home
on weekends to make extra money for statewide chorus
competitions.

Now, Eve's opinion of her mother was one of indifference.
She respected and loved her but at times was unsure of how to
respond to her. It would be three years later the night of Eve's
senior dance, before Eve would know that Mattie did love her. For
the first time Eve was allowed to go to a dance. She, Carolyn, and
Ann had dates. Eve was excited that day and with all the running
around she had a seizure while standing looking at her white lace
gown that hung from her closet door.

Lela heard a thump and ran into her bedroom. Eve was
shaking on the ground. It had been about a year since Eve had a
seizure. Lela had almost thought God had cured her. She ran to Eve
making sure Eve did not injure herself. After about ten minutes Eve
awaken from a deep snoring sleep and Lela helped her to the bed.
Lela troubled by the day's event told Johnny it was no way she was
going to let her go. Eve overhearing their conversation in the next

room began to cry. How would she tell Carolyn, Ann and her date Luke Satchel? She was crying when she heard a knock at the door and someone coming in. It was Mattie who had bought her soft pink heels for the dance. As Mattie walked in Eve's room she saw her daughter's eyes red and swollen.

"Eve what is wrong?" Mattie asked.

"She had a bad spell today. She is not going to the dance." Lela said standing at the edge of the bedroom door.

Mattie looked at Eve and said "I will be right back."

Mattie and Lela went to the next room.

"She is going to the dance, Aunt. She will be fine."

"Mattie, those spells came on her today."

"Has she had anymore today?"

"No, not since this morning."

"She goes to the dance, Aunt."

"Mattie, she . . . "

"She goes because I am her mother and I said so. This time Aunt you will not have your say. She is my child. I gave birth to her, not you, and her mother says she is going to the dance."

Lela looked at Mattie and said "Oh now you want to be a mother, well your Uncle and I have . . . "

"What? Uncle and you have what? Mattie responded.

"I know you both helped me care for Mattie, but no matter what I gave birth to her. I love her. I don't want her life to be a life of what ifs just because of her condition. She is going to the dance. And yes, I guess today if it so please you I decided to be her mother. "

As Mattie walked away, Lela was huffed hearing Mattie tell Eve she was going and she needed to start to get dress. That night Eve went to the dance with Carolyn and Ann. It was the first time Eve was glad that Mattie was her mother and she her daughter.

Chapter 9

Disappointment

The following fall Eve received a scholarship from the Negro college in the city and three years later she worked as a teachers' assistant at the reservation. Eve still sung at reservation events and at church. Eve dated a few guys but nothing serious. She was able to move and get a small flat one block away from Uncle, Aunt and Mattie.

Eve was doing quite well. One day when going to the grocer she noticed the berries and cantaloupes. The reservation was excited to have a new framers market. As Eve walked across the street the first produce she picked up with her hands were oranges. As she was picking up an orange one by one and glazing at them with her big brown eyes a dark skinned man walked up to her and asked "Mam, May I help you?"

Eve looked up to see a man with a beautiful smile she answered "No" with a giggle.

"Do you work here?" Eve asked.

"Well sort of. I am the owner."

"Oh, how exciting!"

"Excuse me mam, I did not get your name?"

"My name is Eve. I heard the reservation was now the home of some new comers"

The man chuckled.

"What is so funny?" Eve asked.

"My name is Mr. Adam Watson."

"Adam and Eve." They both laughed in simultaneously.

Mr. Watson was married with one child. The infamous reservation gossipers noted that Mrs. Hattie Watson was a mean and bitter woman. No one ever knew why Mrs. Watson was so bitter, but that would soon change. She and Mr. Watson had moved into town after Mr. Watson came into some money. He wanted to move to a quiet place and start his own business. Mr. Watson of course loved to say her husband was a fine business man and the reservationists should be forever grateful they chose to build their business on this land.

Anytime Eve came to the market she would speak to Mr. Watson. He knew of Eve's illness from having heard from others on the reservation. Mr. Watson and Eve's talks grew intense and they became familiar and comfortable with each other. So comfortable that one day Eve asked him how was he able to stay with Mrs. Watson.

"Eve, my wife is complex. My wife use to be the kind. She loved me with all she had."

"Did you hurt her Adam?"

"None more than the usual. My wife is angry not with me but with God. Years ago before we came to the reservation there was a great storm of tornadoes. We lost all our children except one. "

"All of your children."

"All three children. The great tornado hit our home. There was nothing we could do. It is by the grace of God my wife; Seth and I are still alive. We all went to the ground for shelter, but the forces of the tornadoes were so great it moved the earth. It uprooted the shelter and flung us all south. We lost our son Adam Jr., and both our daughters Ophelia and Jewel. In one day we buried three of our children.

"Mr. Watson, such great pain. No wonder Mrs. Watson is so angry. It is probably taking all she can just to make it through the day."

"I suppose so." Adam said shyly.

"Oh Adam I did not mean to exclude you. I am sure you are still in pain."

"The pain I live with is like an elephant sitting on my chest. Then I look at Seth and thank God he spared me one child. Hattie on the other hand just can't seem to get passed the hurt. She is very angry with God. "

"I do not talk about it much. So please keep this private."

"Of course I will."

From that day forward Mr. Watson and Eve became the best of friends and every night Eve prayed that Hattie Watson's heart, mind and soul would heal.

The next fall Eve kept her job as a teaching assistant. She was only having one to two seizures a year. The reservationists traveled back and forth to the city by trolley on Saturdays to do some shopping. Eve had met a man in the city name Nicolai. His skin was dark and he was handsome. Nicolai worked in the mill. Nicolai said he had come from New York to visit his brother and found a job as a blacksmith in the city. Every Saturday he would be waiting on Eve to arrive so that they could have lunch. Lela was suspicious at first and nervous that Eve felt no danger in traveling to the city every Saturday, but Eve assured her she was fine. There were at least twenty to thirty other reservationists who went to the city on Saturdays, including Satchel. Lela knew that if anything happened

Satchel would make sure Eve was taken care of. Satchel mentioned once to Lela of a man in the city who seemed to admire Eve but assured Lela that Eve and the young fellow would only meet for lunch. Satchel kept an eye on the both of them in the corner of the Negro restaurant. After about three months of spending almost every Saturday with Nicolai, Eve was able to convince Nicolai to come meet her family. Satchel was please as he did not know how long he could continue to spy on Eve. When Nicolai came for his visit there stood Johnny, Lela, Essie, Mattie, and Matthew waiting. Nicolai was the tallest man they ever seen.

"Come in, Nicolai, heard a lot about you." Uncle Johnny said.

"I have heard about you all. I feel like I know you." Nicolai replied. Lela gave a quaint smile as for some reason she did not particularly like Nicolai.

They all sat around the table and had dinner that Saturday afternoon. Conversation was good and pleasant and Uncle Johnny and Matthew even took Nicolai to see the new wagon Uncle Johnny had bought. Eve was happy as everyone seemed to get along just fine. She began to have grandiose dreams of her and Nicolai getting married and having children. She had not had a seizure in quite some time and Dr. Williams never told her she could not have children. Mattie seemed to like him but Lela had not spoken much during the dinner. Eve thought Lela always behaved this way around people she met for the first time. Nicolai left that night with a smile and Eve was elated they would meet next Saturday at the trolley stop. As Eve went back in the kitchen to help Lela and Mattie cleaned up, Lela said, "He was very vague about his family."

"No he wasn't. He said his parents had died and he had a step brother that lived miles away."

"Mmmm"

"Aunt Lela there you go again. Let Eve be happy." Mattie interrupted.

"Something is wrong. I can see right through him and I see a man who hides in the light."

"Nothing more, Aunt Lela! Nicolai and I have talked about marriage this spring."

As Lela stood in awe, Mattie hugged her daughter to congratulate her.

The following day Lela went immediately knocking on Satchel's door.

"Hello Lela." Dahlia said opening the front door.

"Hello Dahlia." Lela said crying.

"What on earth is wrong?" Dahlia asked.

"I need to speak to Satchel at once."

"Why you come on in. I will get him."

After Lela stood inside the door for a minute there was Satchel.

"Oh, Satchel, Eve is going to marry that man. Something is wrong. I feel it in my gut. How could you let this happen? You were supposed to be keeping an eye on her when she went into the city." Lela said.

"On Lela, you and your gift to see through people is a great gift, but a gift that always has you in an uproar. Don't worry about a thing. They are not married, and besides Eve is an adult. I got a strange feeling the first time I saw that young fellow he would not last long. Don't ask me what it is about, but I got a strange feeling. Now calm down. Go back home and congratulate the newlywed couple.

"Satchel said kissing kissed Lela on the forehead.

"Satchel how am I to act so calm?" Lela asked.

"Trust me Lela, I got a strange feeling. Lela you must remember that God may have given you a gift of intuition, but the storms is God's alone. Now go on home."

"Yes Satchel. I am sorry about my behavior."

"No need to be sorry. You are a woman who cares about her family."

Lela turned around walking home and thinking how on earth she was to remain calm about Eve's upcoming nuptials.

Eve had been extremely happy the next two weeks. She had found her prince charming and better yet she could visit Nicolai and not be spied on by Satchel. Eve thought how silly it was to have Aunt Lela have the old Indian man to spy on her. Eve had begun to spend more time in the city with Nicolai on Saturday. Everything was good until one evening while being held in the arms of Nicolai in his room Eve had a seizure. She shook the bed so fiercely Nicolai thought at first it was an earthquake until he realized nothing else was moving. He was scared to death. He knew of Eve's seizures but had never witnessed one. Nicolai stood in shock standing over Eve watching her sleep and slowly awakening. Eve open her eyes with Nicolai looking at her.

"Nicolai do not worry. It was just a bad spell." Eve spoke with slurred speech.

"But you just shook this bed."

"Nicolai, I have had these spells since I was two years old."

"Eve, the wedding is off. Go back home." Nicolai said in fear.

"What? But I told you about the seizures."

"You need to be home with your family. Rest for a while and on the afternoon trolley go back home." Nicolai said as Eve had now fallen asleep.

When Eve awoken Nicolai was still worried but Eve convinced him everything was fine and she could go home by trolley by herself. Nicolai expressed how concern he was and ask for her forgiveness in reacting so irrationally and calling off the wedding. Eve assured him their life together would be fine. When arriving home by trolley Eve told Uncle Johnny and Aunt Lela about Nicolai and her seizure. They seemed concerned about Eve's carelessness of her illness. Lela could never understand how Eve had no insight into her medical condition. She was always so carefree.

Soon after Eve left Nicolai he immediately packed his belongings and on his way to the train station stopped by the mill to give notice he would not be returning. He told Mr. Peters, his supervisor, he was headed back home to New York. With minutes to spare Nicolai barely caught the last train. As he made his way to his seat and sat by the window he thought of how awful a person he was. He could not have imagined exactly the pain he had caused Eve and his wife. If Eve only knew the truth about him she would know she is much better off without him. While Nicolai pondered these thoughts, a flood of memories how he left his wife and children up north he drifted off to sleep.

The next two weeks Eve went to town but found no Nicolai. She then stopped by Nicolai's room but there was no answer. It was when she went to his job and spoke with Mr. Peters, the supervisor, where she learned Nicolai had left the city for New York two weeks earlier.

Chapter 10

Miracle

Eve was sick to her stomach when she finally realized Nicolai left her. She thought her seizure must have scared him off and how she would never marry or have a family of her own. She became depressed and weak to the point Lela called Dr. Williams. It had been two months since Nicolai disappeared and Eve was not able to eat and when she did she could not keep anything on her stomach. Dr. Williams came along with his son Brock who was in training to become a doctor like his father. The new Dr. Brock Williams confirmed one thing that would have been discovered a little later. Eve's symptoms were more than from a broken heart.

Brock had finished the exam on Eve as his father had come back inside the room after telling Lela and Johnny know that he was assured Eve would be fine. Brock stood up in awe when his father questioned him about what seemed to bother him.

"Nothing Father, I was just asking Eve a few more questions when you left. She is going to be just fine."

Brock and his father left while Eve rested. As both men walked down the hallway to meet Lela and Johnny Brock said in a soft voice.

"Father when you left the room I continued to examine Eve and ask her a few more questions."

"I thought something was strange when I came back inside the room."

"What is it?" Lela asked.

"Eve is pregnant." Brock said.

"Pregnant." Johnny said in dismay.

114

"Did you tell her?" Dr. Williams asked.

"No father, considering her condition and fragile state I thought it best I tell you and Mr. and Mrs. Wyman." Brock said while Essie came through the door.

"Hello everyone, is everything ok?" Essie said

"Yes, Essie everything is fine. Essie take those bags of onion in the kitchen while your father and I talk with Brock and Dr. Williams." Lela replied.

"Yes Mam" Essie responded as she rolled her eyes at Brock who was smiling at her.

"Mr. & Mrs. Wyman I believe the conversation you are going to have with my father is one of great concern. I hope you don't mind I need to speak with Essie briefly." Brock said to Lela and Johnny.

"Yes, son you go on ahead I can further tell Lela and Johnny what to do from this point on." Dr. Williams replied as all nodded in agreement.

"We are going to have to tell her and soon. For now we will let her rest. Lela the portion I gave her should settle her stomach and will not harm the baby. But remember her situation and this pregnancy is delicate."

As Dr. Williams continued to speak Brock had now made his way to the kitchen to speak with Essie.

"Hello Essie." Brock said.

"Hello Brock, what do you want?" Essie asked in a disdained voice.

"You know what I want. When will you be my lady?"

"Never."

"You still mad about the spanking in school you got when you told me to kiss that chicken when we were little I see." Brock smiled.

"If I may ask how is Susan Foster? Talk is you two are hot and heavy." Essie responded.

"Now Essie, you know it don't mean nothing."

"Did you tell her that?"

"Essie you still owe me a kiss."

"Tall, dark, black wavy hair and you Dr. Brock Williams looking as handsome as ever. Just to think you made it back home from medical school to have the women just swoon all over you and yet, I would not touch you with a broomstick." Essie replied sarcastically.

"Why look at you Essie Mae? Your red curls so tight with your choke collar dress you should be happy any man wants to speak to you. You are going to grow to become an old prude Essie Wyman if you don't change that your high and mighty attitude." Brock said.

"First of all Dr. Brock Williams how shameful for you to be talking that way to me in my parents' home, and secondly I will never be your girlfriend. Unlike Susan Foster I am wife material so you can take your puckered lips and kiss your chicken." Essie said with her hands on her hips.

"Baby if that was all you wanted all you have to do is kiss me and I will marry you."

"I believe that lie when pigs fly."

"Essie Wyman maybe not today or tomorrow but you are going to give me a kiss and be my girlfriend one day."

"Just like I thought. You are using the girlfriend speech on a woman who is wife material. It is never going to work." Essie replied.

With that being said Brock smiled and returned to leave with his father. Essie Wyman and Dr. Brock Williams were married the next year.

"Thank you both for coming." Lela said as Brock returned to the conversation.

"Don't worry about a thing. You all just rest." Dr. Williams said as Johnny escorted him and Brock to the door.

Lela and Johnny stood and stared at each other when they heard a knock at the door.

Johnny opened the door to find Satchel standing.

"Hello Johnny and Lela. Just came by to see how songbird was doing." Satchel said.

"You told me she would be just fine, but everything is not fine." Lela cried.

"What is wrong with her Johnny?" Satchel asked.

"Eve is pregnant. Dr. Williams and his son just told us. Eve does not know just yet. She is in her room resting." Johnny answered.

"Now, Lela stop worrying about so much." Satchel said as he placed his hands on Lela's shoulders and looked her in the face. "God has a way of performing miracles in the midst of some of his greatest storms. "

The next morning, Johnny and Lela told Eve of the pregnancy. When Eve heard of the pregnancy she became happy. The pregnancy seemed to take her mind of off the loss of Nicolai. Johnny decided to go to New York and try and find Nicolai but he had no such luck. It seemed no one heard of him. It was almost as if Nicolai had disappeared from the face of the earth.

Fortunately, Eve was still able to work cleaning the home of Mrs. Jackson, formerly Mrs. Crawford, after marrying a prominent business man from the city. Eve managed to finish the teacher's assistant position for the school term. Fortunately, Eve did not show during her pregnancy. She saved every penny she had. Since discovering the pregnancy she had not been back to see Adam at the grocer. She just worked and went home. Her focused was this child and her thoughts of becoming a mother. Mattie seemed indifferent about the pregnancy as she was not happy to become a grandmother. She showed Eve no compassion and barely spoke to her.

One day Eve was coming to sit on the screen porch to talk with Johnny when she seemed to get a little dizzy.

"Is everything ok, Eve?" Johnny asked.

"Yes, everything is fine." Eve said when suddenly she fell to the ground.

"Lela! Essie! Help!" Johnny screamed as he ran to a fallen shaking Eve. Eve body shook for only a few seconds. By the time Essie and Lela came running the spell was over. They call Dr. Williams immediately. When he came, there lay Eve in the bed. He gave her an examination while Johnny and Lela stood in the room with fear and trembling. Dr. Williams assured everyone he could still here the baby's heartbeat. It seemed everything was fine. As he left the room he asked for Johnny and Lela to speak with him outside.

"Johnny and Lela, I don't know about Eve carrying this child. We are just going to have to pray. Everything seems fine but her seizures can come on her at any moment. It is possible Eve and this child could have problems."

"What do you mean Doc?" Johnny asked.

"Well let's just say we are going to have to keep a close eye on Eve. Her condition is delicate due to her epilepsy. "

"I know I have been worried about her condition. I have been praying and praying." Lela said.

"I just wanted you to know this pregnancy is a dangerous situation."

"Yes, sir." Johnny and Lela said in unison.

Eve was on bed rest for the duration of the pregnancy. Everyone was on pins and needle except her. She had made the baby a lovely crotchet blanket and though she missed Nicolai Eve became more excited by the day of becoming a mother. It did not matter what she had to do to have this child, Eve was content. Eve's pregnancy was long and hard but after forty-seven hours of labor Eve bore a daughter. The child was name Maria Elizabeth. She was adored at birth. From what Dr. Williams and Dr. Brock Williams could gather child and mother were healthy. Satchel came by one day after hearing about the new addition to the reservation.

"Hello Satchel." Lela said as she hugged Satchel.

"Lela, everything is fine."

"Yes, Satchel everything is fine. Johnny went to work at the mills tonight so he is not home."

"Well, I came by to see our newest little citizen. Like I always do on the reservation at every birth I come to give the child a spiritual name."

"Yes, that is the tradition we have on this land." Lela smiled.

As Satchel made his way to see the baby while Lela followed, he stopped, and turned to her and said, "See Lela, I told you God always performs a miracle in the midst of some of his greatest storms."

Part III

The Thunder Storms of God

Chapter 11

Truth

My name is Maria Elizabeth. I am a descendant of the Indian Negro reservation governed by the Great Chief Satchel. My mother said when Satchel performed the ceremonial blessing of my birth he looked into my eyes, shook his head and named me "Miracle". As I grew my mother was able to continue to work at the reservation school and Aunt Lela took care of me until I was school age. I had monthly visits doctor visits to see Cousin Brock as he kept a close watch on my health to see if I had seizures. My Aunt Lela said "God had smile on me and I was the perfect child." My skin is pecan tan. My hair is soft as wool and black as an Indian. The white iris of my eyes can be seen in the dark and more importantly I have never been sick. One day when I was only a few months old my mother decided to take me for a walk in my stroller. During our walk she stopped by the grocer since she had not been anywhere in months. There she saw her dear friend, Adam.

"Eve, good to see you. I thought you ran off when you got married. I have not seen you in months. I heard about the baby. Have you and your husband decided to move back here on the reservation." Adam smiled.

"No, the marriage did not quite work out but I was left a little package."

As he bent over to see me he said, "Eve she is beautiful. "

"Well she will never know her father. Seems he ran off."

"Eve, I am so sorry."

"How are you Adam?"

Adam looked down at the ground.

"What is wrong?" Eve asked.

"My wife is very ill."

"I am so sorry Adam."

"The bitterness and pain that ate away at her heart has taken over her body."

"I will pray for her." Eve said gently touching Adam's right hand.

"Eve who was the man who stole your heart?"

"Nicolai was his name. He saw me have a seizure one day and left but not before I could tell him of the baby. "

"Nicolai!" Adam said shockingly.

"Yes, do you know him? He was here visiting his step brother and worked for about a five months as a blacksmith in the city."

"Eve, I am Nicolai's step brother."

"Adam do you know where he is? "

"Eve come to my office now."

As the two walked back to the office with me in stroller Adam closed the door.

"Have a seat Eve." Adam said pulling out a chair.

"Where is Nicolai?"

"I don't know how to tell you this." Adam said while he kneeled at Eve's side and took her hand. "Eve my step brother is from the second marriage of my father. Nicolai was always a hand full. When he left here he had been planning to go back up north to be his wife Ann and his two daughters."

"He was already married."

"I am afraid so."

Eve cried in despair.

"Furthermore as he was traveling by train it derailed twenty miles outside of New York." As Adam took Eve's hand he said "Eve, Nicolai is dead."

"Why didn't you tell me?" Eve screamed and cried.

"Eve you stop coming here on Saturdays. I did not know anything. He never visited me while he was here other than once to ask for money. He never mentioned you. I would have told you had I known. Believe me."

Eve said softly through her tears "I believe you. Well at least I know what has happened. Could you do me a favor and say nothing to no one."

"I would never betray you. I will not say a word."

Eve was flushed and disturbed but eased at the fact that she knew the truth. As Eve arose from the chair there was a knock on the door.

"Come in." Adam said as he stood.

"Adam it seems as if someone knocked over your tomato stand." Satchel said.

"I will be right there." Adam replied.

"Hello Songbird." Satchel said to Eve.

"Hello Satchel."

"Why songbird is everything ok? You look rather perplex."

"Everything is fine."

"I see that bundle of joy you have there. She is pretty. Why her eyes are as black as my mother's eyes."

Eve smiled.

"Well see you later songbird." Satchel said walking away while mumbling under his breath "God, help Eve."

"Good day Satchel." Eve replied. As Eve walked home with me in stroller it was at that very moment she decided to never speak again of Nicolai to anyone.

From that day on Eve went to the grocer every Saturday and her and Mr. Watson would have their weekly chat. It would still be years before Mrs. Watson died and before the relationship between Eve and Adam would flourish.

Chapter 12

Peace

As the years passed Essie took care of Aunt Lela and Uncle Johnny. Uncle Matthew and Uncle Johnny Jr. would come to dinner with their wives on Sundays, and Grandma Mattie came over on Saturdays mornings to spend time with me while mother would go to the grocer. The Crawfords would come every Saturday at noon and bring milk for me and on occasions Satchel would pass by the home and I would wave to him and he back to me.

Mr. Crawford and I would play for hours and I became attach to him as a child would her father. When I became four years of age the Crawford's paid for me to attend a school during the summer in the city for black gifted children. Mrs. Crawford would pick me up every morning by wagon. The school hours were only eight a.m. to noon but during those hours we not only learned ABC's and 123's, we learned to read Shakespeare and appreciate the music of Bach and Beethoven. We learned of the rise and fall of the Roman Empire and memorized the love poems of Songs of Solomon. Mr. and Mrs. Crawford would return by wagon at one o'clock pm. and we would come back to the reservation and fish for the remaining day on the pond. It was a peaceful time. I remember we talked about everything from frogs, worms, fig trees and God. Often Mr. Crawford looked into Mrs. Crawford eyes with love. I even remember one conversation in particular.

Mr. Crawford said solemnly "Sweetie I want to be buried on my birthday."

"What a strange thing to say, honey."

"What I am saying is would it not be nice to go back to heaven on the same day you came on earth?"

"I guess so." Mrs. Crawford replied.

"Sweetie I love you." Mr. Crawford said dearly.

"I love you too."

"I love you both." I said to both of them.

"We love you." Mr. and Mrs. Crawford said in unison.

"We need to be getting on back." Mr. Crawford said as he stood up with his fishing rod.

"We better be going. The fish aren't biting today anyway." Mrs. Crawford agreed.

Mrs. Crawford packed up our picnic basket. She stood up and walked away to put the basket in the wagon while Mr. Crawford was getting the fishing rods. As he stood I will never forget he grabbed his chest with a painful facial expression but made no noise. I looked at him and held his other hand. After about three seconds the pain must have been gone as he looked at me and manage to give me a small smile. Little did I know that day would mark the beginning of the treacherous storms that would change all our lives.

Chapter 13

Inheritance

The following Saturday my mother left to go visit Mr. Watson at the grocer's market but he was not there. Satchel was there running the store.

"Hello, Songbird."

"Hello, Satchel."

"Need anything."

"No Satchel. I needed to speak with Adam about something."

"Oh, I see." Satchel said.

"Do you know where he is?"

"Yes. It seems Mrs. Watson has taken a turn for the worse. She is not expected to live till tomorrow. That cancer has taken over her entire body. She is in extreme pain. I am going to run the market for a while until Watson can manage."

"Oh my goodness. Poor Adam." Eve sighed.

Eve stood still and just for a moment thought of what Adam must be going through. She walked back home in disbelief. Before the nightfall came, news of Mrs. Watson's death rang throughout the reservation.

It would be a month later before Eve would see Adam again. It was a Sunday morning and my mother, Essie, Aunt Lela had just come from Sunday church service. We were all headed up the stairs to the porch when Mr. Watson rode by on wagon. As Mr. Watson jumped out of the wagon mother asked "Why Adam what is wrong?"

"Got a message from Mr. Steele at the post office. Telegraph came in for you Eve. Mr. Crawford has taken ill. He is in the city hospital. Mrs. Crawford needs you to come immediately."

As my mother went to leave I screamed for her so she decided to take me despite Aunt Lela's protest. In arriving in the city we went immediately to the Negro hospital. I remember the glass double doors and the sleek and shiny floors. I remember my mother Eve was in tears. As we made our way through the hallways Mr. Watson directed my mother and I up the stairs and to the room of Mr. Crawford. There he lay in peace.

"Mr. Crawford it's me, it's Eve and Maria."

Mr. Crawford opened his eyes and said, "Let me see my baby."

"My mother pushed me up to the bed and Mr. Watson picked me up and I leaned over and Mr. Crawford kissed me on the cheek and said I love you."

"I love you too." I said.

"Eve listen carefully. I have a small home in the city. It was the home of me and my first wife Abigail. At one time she lived on the old reservation with her first husband Pastor Wright. She died of rheumatic fever years ago. I have it in the papers that you are to have that home. This home will give you and Maria a place to stay in the city where the child can have a better opportunity for her schooling."

"I can't. . ."

"It is done and Grace approves. Eve I love you." He said as he closed his eyes to rest.

"I love you too." My mother cried.

My mother and I left the room and Mrs. Crawford stood in the corner of the room watching her husband sleep. That evening Mr. Watson took us back home and my mother told Aunt Lela and Uncle Johnny of Mr. Crawford's gift.

Aunt Lela looked in amazement and said "What kind of gesture is this? I guess you and this child were the children he never had."

"He said it was the home of him and his first wife Abigail. He said she use to live on the old reservation land."

My Aunt Lela just sat in her chair and did not say a word. Johnny looked at Lela and showed no emotion. My mother left the room as she was busy getting our clothes in order for the next day. My Aunt Lela looked at me and said "Child, all these years and I thought God had forgot something. Looked like he remembered after all. Let's get to bed. I hear a thunder."

"Amen." Uncle Johnny said.

That night I could not sleep. I was not frightened. I just kept looking around in the dark looking through the window curtains from my bed and hearing the sounds of thunder. The next day was no summer school since parts of the city were flooded. By that afternoon Mr. Watson came by and said another telegraph had come and Mr. Crawford had died. Within four days we had the funeral. Mother, I, Mr. Watson, Essie, Cousin Brock, Grandma Mattie, Aunt Lela and Uncle Johnny were all there. There Mr. Crawford lay in a mahogany casket in his favorite shiny blue gray suite, white crisp shirt with matching blue strip tie.

That same day Mrs. Crawford gave my mother a key to the small home. I t was a nice home. Mr. Crawford had been making repairs when he died. According to Mr. Watson he was able to finish most of the work.

The house was white with a black painted wooden door panels and a red door. It was a small five room house with a backyard. The grass was green and most importantly there was a fig and apple tree outback.

"Eve, I can finish the repairs." Mr. Watson said.

I could not tell what repairs Watson was speaking off. Sure the furnishings were covered in plastic and things were a bit dusty but the house seemed perfect.

"Then you can sell it." Aunt Lela said while Uncle Johnny looked at my mother to hear of her opinion.

"I am not selling it." Eve said.

"Eve you cannot stay here by yourself with your seizures. What about Maria?" Aunt Lela questioned.

"I will be fine. Anyway I can keep the home and use it for borders."

"Now that is not a bad idea. There have been a lot of blacks lately moving to the city. Sometimes even the hotel is full." Uncle Johnny chimed.

For the next weeks there was discussion about the home but I was always told to leave the room. My mother decided to keep the home. My mother, Mr. Watson, Uncle Johnny, Satchel, Timothy Cook, Elder Dubose, and myself would come to the city on Saturday mornings. It seemed we would make repairs, paint, and receive shipments of fabric. After about four months Cousin Essie and Aunt Lela came to see the home. I was hoping Aunt Lela liked the home now that it was completed.

"Oh, Eve this is wonderful." Aunt Essie smiled.

"It's pretty." Aunt Lela said sarcastically.

The following summer my mother Eve seemed to have a strange cough that persisted all summer into the fall. I remembered the day it started. It was a Saturday and my mother and I were cleaning the house. I was outside sweeping the porch when my mother summoned for me to come in for supper. I notice my mother had been coughing all that morning.

"You sick, Ma?" I asked.

"No child. I am fine. I must have gotten a little bug. Nothing to concern yourself about. Go wash up for supper." My mother replied.

It was that evening and all during supper my mother had a terrible cough. I dare not suggest to my mom that we call Aunt Lela because my mother was determined to live on her own. But as the summer progress and Mr. Watson and others notice this cough did not seem to be going away. Cousin Brock and Dr. Williams had been to examine my mother.

I remember like it was yesterday. Aunt Lela, Uncle Johnny, Cousin Essie, Grandma Mattie and Mr. Watson all stood outside the room waiting on a verdict. Aunt Lela had summoned me to my room but I had managed to sneak outside the door to hear what was wrong with my mother.

"I knew I should have made her come back to the reservation. This damn house kept her away from us. "Aunt Lela said.

"Lela calm down. Eve is grown and she can make decisions on her own. You always get yourself in a worry every time this family goes through a crisis. Lela that is life and I am sick and tired of the complaining and nagging. I want you to be quiet when Brock and

Doc Williams come out of the room. I mean it." Uncle Johnny spoke in one of the sternest voices I had ever heard.

The examination seemed to have taken hours. Cousin Brock and Dr. Williams finally came out of the room and gave Aunt Lela some medicines to get from the druggist.

"It is quite bad. It seems she has a lung infection of some sort. These medicines may work and then again they may not. She may live and then again she may die. Only time will tell. All we can do at this point is pray and hope." Dr. Williams said to everyone in the room. I stood outside that door frozen in time. From that moment on I had no feeling.

The next two weeks were difficult as the medicines seemed to have no effect on my mother's condition. Finally my mother had to be taken to the city hospital when one morning she simply could not grasp her breath. After about one week it was determine that my mother's lung infection was no better and again only time could tell the outcome of her fate.

Mr. Watson had begun to come by every Saturday to visit and spend time with my mother. Mrs. Crawford stayed with my mother during the week and Cousin Essie, Aunt Lela, Uncle Johnny, Grandma Mattie, and I visited the hospital every Saturday. Satchel and the other elders would stop by on occasions when they had to come to the city on business. I could never figure out what business would bring the elders to the city but in time I would come to know Satchel's and the elders' secret. My mother stayed in the hospital for about three months. It was a surprise to me when Uncle Johnny told Lela that Eve should stay at home in the city. It was closest to the hospital. For the first time ever Aunt Lela made no rumbling sound and agreed with her husband. My mother was able to stay in her home after all. Mrs. Crawford now retired from the reservation school would care for my mother during the day and I would care for my mother at night. I was seven years of age and I thought I was practically an adult. Aunt Lela and Uncle Johnny though strong were getting on in years and it took all Essie could do to care for them; however, they would come every Sunday afternoon.

Mr. Watson began to even come during the week which gave me time to complete my homework, cook our meals, sweep the floors, clean the house, wash clothes, and finish my chores. My mother's illness was taking a toll on my childhood. I did not have many friends and felt at times my mother's illness had become my imprisonment. Her back and forth to the hospital persisted and it was a difficult time for us all.

"Good morning" I said as I entered her bedroom with her Saturday morning breakfast.

My mother looked at me, sat up in the bed and smiled slowly.

"I think I will walk today."

"Are you sure you can? Besides, Watson should be here soon. Maybe you should wait for him."

As my mother took a sip of the tea I prepared I looked into her eyes and asked, "Mother, where is my father?"

"Maria what would make you asks such a thing?"

"The other day Mrs. Crawford came to the school to pay my tuition and one of the girls at the school asked why doesn't my dad pay my tuition like all the other children's fathers? I told her I didn't know anything about my father. I had never thought of it before, but where is he, mother?"

"Your father died in a train accident before you were born."

"If you die where do I go?"

"Well, to tell you the truth I never really thought about it but that is because I never thought I was going to die. Everyone else may have thought I would not have long on this earth, but as for me it never entered my mind."

"Never?" I asked.

"Maria, no matter my illness, I am going to be right here to see you grow. I promise. The grace of God and you is what keeps me breathing. "

"Yes mam." I replied taking the breakfast tray back to the kitchen. I then thought to myself my mother must be delusional. All of the trips to the hospitals and doctors with no definite answer on her condition and never did she think she would die. Her faith in God was greater than what I could imagine.

Other than that revelation, the day was uneventful. That night the thunder storms came again. Alone in my bed after just checking in on mother I watch through the curtains of the shadows of darkness and heard the thunders of God. The next day as I returned from school, Cousin Essie had stopped by to help me with some of the cooking. Essie had promise me she would surprise me by making my favorite, lemon pound cake. Essie and I were in the kitchen mixing the cake batter. She had just given me a small bowl of batter to enjoy. As I went to turn around I did not realize the kitchen table was in front of me and dropped the bowl with batter on the floor.

"Damn!" I said.

"What you say?" Essie replied. "What is wrong with you child?"

I looked at Essie with my cold black eyes and tears stream down my cheeks.

"Maria, come here. Now tell me what is going on with you." Essie said as I sat in her lap.

"I could not sleep last night Essie. The thunderstorms were scary." I cried.

"Now Maria, don't cry and that is no excuse to curse. Besides the thunder is God speaking to us loudly when he really needs his children to hear what he has to say. That is his way of letting us know he is in control. Do you understand Maria?"

"Yes, Mam." I replied.

"You must learn that some of the most beautiful experiences in life come for our most painful hardships." Essie said.

"Yes, mam."

"Ok. Now say your prayers, ask God for grace, and mercy, and go to bed."

"Yes mam."

Just as I went to get up from the table there was Satchel.

"Hello Essie. I did not mean to startle you all this late evening. I knocked at the door but no one answered. I was getting a little worried so I came on in."

"Satchel everything is fine. What brings you here?"

"You know I have been working on this elixir from the vines of some of the plants on the reservation for quite some time. Give some to Songbird and see if this will make her rest better."

"Will do Satchel and thank you."

"If it does her good, I will make some more." Satchel said. "Hello." Satchel continued.

"Hello Satchel."

"Well I need to be getting back to the reservation and I believe Miracle should be getting to bed." Satchel said with a smile as he turned and walked out of the house.

"Let me walk you to the door Satchel. I need to speak with you about something." Essie said.

I returned to my bed as Essie walked Satchel to the door.

"Satchel, be careful." Essie said.

"Essie you are just glowing like a new mother."

"Finally, I am pregnant. Brock does not know yet. I have not told anyone but you, Satchel."

"Don't worry my child. I will pray and everything will be fine."

"Thank you Satchel." Essie said as Satchel walked away smiling.

Later on that night I ask God for grace and mercy just as I was told and I went to bed. I lay there with my eyes open. For a moment it seemed as if the world had stop. As I went to shut my eyes a cool breeze fell over my face. I gently raised my head and looked around to see if anyone was there, but saw no one. I laid back down in my bed still thinking about what Cousin Essie had told me about the thunderstorms. I realize God was powerful. At that moment another cool breeze fell over my face. I raised my head again but saw no one. As I lay down slowly I thought if the thunderstorms are the voice of God when he speaks loudly then maybe the cool breeze is the voice of God when he speaks in a whisper. That was the first night since my mother's illness I slept in peace.

Chapter 14

Happiness

As the years passed Cousin Essie's and Brock's son, Cecil grew to be like his father always trying to kiss the girls, Grandma Mattie and I became close, and my mother slowly regained her health. Satchel's elixir seemed to help my mother get better but not at a record pace. Her recovery had become like a slow healing wound. Nevertheless, it was a healing and the family was grateful.

I was now all grown up and had been accepted to the college for Negroes in the city. My first year of schooling was not a great challenge as I thought. I seemed to do quite well and actually made a few friends. Grandma Mattie was now getting on in age and moved in with Uncle Johnny and Aunt Lela.

Watson would come by and he and my mother would talk for hours. He had become part of the family. My mother's relationship with Watson had progressed into more than a friendship. Like my mother's healing, their love had also grown slowly. Nevertheless, it was love and the family was grateful.

The wedding took place on a Sunday afternoon. The family came and Mrs. Crawford sung "Ave Maria" as my mother made her way to the rose garden in our back yard. Their stood my mother for the first time in a white Chantilly lace gown and Mr. Watson in a black suit smiling. My mother and Mr. Watson honeymoon in the next big city for just two days. Mr. Watson sold his business and moved to the city to be with my mother. On a few occasions I met Mr. Watson's son, Seth. Seth was now married and living in California and had become a lawyer. His son seemed pleased to have his father find happiness. When they returned I decided it was best I stay on the college campus in the women's living quarters.

Life on campus was very different. I had freedom to live my life. My depression and loneliness seemed to fade while I was either busy studying or grading papers. Like all the other women in my family I wanted to become a teacher, but the next two years events in my life would take my steps into an unforeseen journey. It began one summer during my junior year in college when I got a job at the Negro hospital as a secretary, file clerk and lab assistant. Many of the staff worked many occupations at the hospital.

It was there at the hospital during the summer I blossom. I was becoming acquainted with the staff. The staff had become my second family. One night just as I was about to leave for the evening David Long, one of the hospital maintenance workers walked in with a pregnant hemorrhaging woman.

I ran to get a gurney as fast as possible and called out for help.

"David, what on earth has happened?" I asked.

"This is my wife, Amelia. She is about eight months pregnant. We were eating dinner and she told me something was wrong and to get her to the hospital. I brought her here as fast as I could. She just started bleeding as soon as we walked through the door."

By this time Dr. Pleasant had made his way to assure David everything would be fine and he, Nurse Martha and Nurse Celia rushed away with Amelia now lying helplessly, bleeding on the gurney.

"Don't worry David. Everything will be fine. We just need to pray."

"No. Something is very wrong. Something is very wrong." David replied while he looked at me with a fear in his eyes.

"Well I am going to stay right here with you. You shouldn't be alone at a time like this."

David and I waited in the hallway for at least two hours. During that time I mop the entry way, made him some coffee, and did all I could to assure him everything would be fine. During that time Mr. Bice, David's supervisor, and other staff members who were leaving for the evening saw him and decided they all should wait with David. Those two hours lingered as if weeks had passed and then we saw Dr. Pleasant walking towards David.

"We did all we could." Dr. Pleasant said while David burst into tears. "We could not save Amelia."

"What about the baby?" I asked.

"The baby pulled through. It was touch and go for a while and she is small for her size but she is alive. David you have a daughter."

David, standing in shock became quite somber and the staff put their arms around him.

For the next few months we did as any family would do. Everyone brought diaper cloths, dresses, quilts, a bassinet and all the baby stuff in the world we thought he would need. It wasn't anything David Long's baby did not have. During those months David and I spoke a few times in passing. After about eight months David's mother came to the hospital with the baby to deliver some items David had manage to get for the hospital from a doctor friend of his who lived up north. As she entered a few of the workers were excited to see the child. After a few minutes of standing in the entry way his mother went to pass my desk as David was coming to the end of the hall. His mother looked at me and asked, "Do you want to see her?"

"Yes, Mam." I said walking around the desk and there was the white basket with the child. The child was beautiful while making cooing sounds.

"Hello mother, have you met Maria?" David asked.

"Yes, she was just looking at Elise." His mother replied.

"She is beautiful David." I chimed.

"Yes she is." David replied

As his mother handed David the package and left with Elise I sat down at my desk completing some paperwork. Something was strange with David. He seemed to be paralyzed while staring at me.

"David is everything ok?" I asked.

"Maria, would you like to have lunch sometimes?"

"Of course David."

"Maybe this Saturday at the Inn at noon."

"I will be there." I said. I thought to myself it would be nice to have lunch and cheer up a friend.

That Saturday David and I met for lunch. It was pleasant and peaceful. I told every joke I knew to cheer him up and he seemed to laugh during the entire meal. We talk for about an hour before he had to get back to his mother and Elise. It was from that day on every Saturday we had lunch at noon at the inn. One Saturday I was surprise to see Satchel. He had come to the city to buy some supplies needed for the new addition of the church.

"Hello Miracle."

"Satchel", I said as I leaped from my chair to hug him. "Meet my friend David Long."

"Nice to meet you sir." David said as he stood to shake Satchel's hand.

"Nice to meet you as well. It seems from the smile on her face my Miracle is happy."

"Yes, sir."

"Well good. Everyone in life needs a Miracle. You two get back to your lunch."

As Satchel walked away, David leaned across the table to ask me in a whisper

"Why does he call you Miracle?"

"That is my name given to me during my blessing on entering the earth. The Chief gives all the newborns a blessed name.

"Why, that is quite different."

"Chief Satchel teaches us that the people on the reservation are different." I smiled.

"Would you to come back with me to my home and see Elise?" David asked.

"Oh, David I would be thrill." I said.

That afternoon he and I took Elise for a walk. It was a beautiful afternoon and from that day on David, Elise, and I were inseparable. After about a year things seemed to going along well as David and I had now spoken of marriage. I remember as if it was only yesterday as David and I sat on the swing of his front porch and I asked, "David am I a blessing to you?"

"Why of course." David replied.

"And you and Elise are a blessing to me."

"Maria, what about marriage?"

"What about it?"

"No, I mean you and me."

"Oh, David, I would be honored to be your wife and the mother of your children."

"There is something though I need to tell you."

"What would that be?"

"Before my wife died I felt I had a calling from God to become a minister."

"David, I know a lot has happened in your life but if God told you to become a minister than you must. You must trust God." I responded.

"Mmmm."

That evening after our conversation as I made my way back to my flat I prayed for God to help David and keep him safe. After about a week David had taken study under a local minister in the city. He was excited and I was excited for him. David seemed to have a great passion and fervent love for God. I was bewildered and in love, but all would soon change.

Chapter 15

Forgiveness

During the next few months I was afforded the opportunity to begin work as an assistant to the Negro druggist in the city. My degree in biology and knowing the use of some plants persuaded Mr. McComb to overlook the fact that I was a woman. In addition, Mr. McComb had been trying for years to extrapolate the formulas of Satchel's miracle drugs. Satchel would sell his medicines to the hospital and others who had bad burns, cuts, and breathing problems. Satchel had a total of three medicines that seemed to be making talk throughout the medical community, but of course Satchel would never tell the ingredients. Mr. McComb was hoping maybe being from the reservation that I either knew of Satchel's formulas or that me working with him would make Satchel more incline to finally revealed his extracts, but Satchel never spoke a word to Mr. McComb when he stop by from time to time to see me.

"Good evening Miracle." Satchel said walking into the druggist store.

Before I could respond Mr. McComb had ran from the back of the store.

"Why it is the great Indian Satchel. It is always so good to see you." Mr. McComb interrupted.

"Mmmm. Miracle when is the wedding?" Satchel asked while ignoring Mr. McComb.

"Why we haven't set a date, but I am sure in a few months." I answered.

"You know Miracle I was thinking about some things that happened in my life when I was younger." Satchel said.

"Why do tell?" Mr. McComb answered with enthusiasm.

"If you could please excuse yourself Mr. McComb, I am talking to Miracle."

"Oh, sorry to interrupt. You two go right ahead. I will just be in the back room." Mr. McComb said smiling and walking away.

"He is annoying. He always tries to be my friend to get the secrets of my medicines. As I was saying Miracle, I remembered a time in my life where I had a moment of great joy to be happening at a time of great pain."

"What are you saying to me Satchel?"

"Just remember, when a man has great joy added to great pain that equals great confusion in his life."

"Ok Satchel. I will remember that." I said while smiling.

Immediately, after that visit from Satchel, David became even busier with his studies until something changed on a cold February Monday morning.

I had not seen David in a month and one day while going to work I decided to stop by the hospital to visit. As I made my way through the double doors I went to the front desk and ask for David. The young lady was polite as she left the station and within minutes there was David. I was happy to see him and hugged him with joy. Not only did he not seem pleased to see me but He immediately asked to see me outside.

"Look I was going to tell you but we cannot get married."

"What do you mean? What is going on?"

"I love her."

"You love who."

"You know I have to do what is best for me and Elise."

I stood still and with a sadness remembering what Satchel had told me that day at Mr. McCombs pharmacy. Then I said "David, God sent me to be your wife. You are making the biggest mistake of your life, but neither God nor I can make you do what you do not want to. Goodbye." And as I turned with my head held high the tears from my face fell to the ground and I never looked back. I could only think how I was there to be with him during the saddest time of his life and how I felt betrayed. I thought of conversations we shared and how he read his first sermon to me. I thought how Elise would grow to think I had left her. Never knowing it was not my choice. I told no one. When Mr. Watson and mom asked about David I said the wedding is off and I do not want to hear the name again. A few of my friends at the hospital knew of me and David but they never inquired about what happened and I did not bother to tell. Within three months David married a woman named Sophia who was a mother of three children. Fortunately David had to be to work much early than my walk to the druggist so I did not have to contend with seeing him; however, one morning I saw Mr. Fred Bice, David's supervisor.

"Maria, is that you?"

"Yes, Mr. Bice it is good to see you."

"Maria you look beautiful. Why if I was not married I make you mine."

"Thank you Mr. Bice." I said as I gave him a small peck on the cheek. Just at that moment I could see David walking up out of the corner of my eye. I said, "Good day." turning and going to work.

"Good day, Maria." Mr. Bice replied.

I cried for months to myself as I felt alone once again. One Saturday Mr. Watson, mom and I went to the reservation to visit Uncle Johnny and Aunt Lela. It was always nice to be with them. As everyone went on with their conversations I could not stop thinking of my dreams deferred. I stood outside waving to Ms. Emma while she sat on her front porch where I saw Satchel. I wave to him but this time he nodded to me as he had a bag of groceries in one hand and a walking stick in the other hand. Uncle Johnny sat and saw him from the porch and he said, "Maria, go help the old Indian. He knows he should not be carrying all that stuff. Besides he told me the other day he needed to speak with you. "

I ran as fast as I could to Satchel and said as I took the bag, "Satchel let me help you with those things. You know you should not be carrying all this stuff. I will walk with you. Uncle Johnny said you needed to speak with me."

"Never had a lady to carry my bags." Satchel smiled as I laughed. Satchel continued, "Miracle it is good to hear you laugh. Shouldn't you be married?"

"Didn't work out."

"Oh, sorry to hear that."

"Well he moved on with someone else."

"Is that why your eyes have lost their light?" Satchel asked.

"Maybe so." I responded shrugging my shoulders. "Satchel, can I ask you something?"

"Sure."

"Why do people mislead others?"

"Miracle, people don't mislead others. People mislead themselves."

"I don't understand."

"To hurt others is to cut God's blessing for your life. Now, I was not going to say anything but you know people talk. Your beau now a preacher done married this other woman."

"Satchel, how do you know?"

"This old Indian knows a lot."

"I guess you do."

"Miracle, listen to the old Satchel for a moment. You did nothing wrong. You loved as God created you to do. "

"I miss his daughter Elise calling me "Ma" "

"That child called you Ma?" Satchel asked shockingly.

"Yes." I replied.

"Then that settles everything I had been meaning to ask you. When that child called you "Ma", he was supposed to stop looking for his wife. It is simple. God had answered his prayers. People often miss hearing from God because He does not tell us what we want to hear. "

"But Satchel I am sure he prayed on his decision to marry Sophia."

"Sweetie, sometimes people can pray all night long and still get it wrong. See most of the time the answer to your prayers was always there before the prayer was prayed."

"Is that why you told me when a man has great joy added with great pain that equals to great confusion."

"Yes, and before his life is over he will make even more poor decisions until he understands that this is God's world and no amount of manipulation we do as people is going to change the ways of God. "

"What do I do now Satchel?" I asked sadly.

"Forgive. Forgiveness not only frees you but places the other person totally in God's hands and when you forgive, give yourself time to heal. Promise me you want do anything irrational. I have seen women burn up clothes, burn down houses, and once I recall burn the man himself. " Satchel said in disbelief.

"No Satchel, I want behave irrational. I promise."

"Good. You must remember in life no matter what a person does to hurt you, you must never throw a stone that you can't bear the pain of getting hit with yourself. Throw some forgiveness there way and God will throw a miracle your way." Satchel said smiling.

"That reminds me Satchel I heard Uncle Johnny and Aunt Lela talking of you getting into a fight with Jesse Sanders boy. Is it true?" I asked shockingly.

"That nine year old boy is a nuisance. He was throwing rocks at some of the girls one day at the school while I was bringing a package to Ms. Sides, the teacher, and one of those rocks hit me in the arm. When he saw he had hit me he looked me in my eyes, turned and began to run. I politely picked up the same rock he had hit me with and belted him in the bottom."

"Well, they say Mr. Sanders heard about it and beat his hide. "

"Mmmm" Satchel moaned.

"Satchel didn't you name him "Peacemaker" at his blessing?" I asked in a questioning tone.

"I must have been drunk during that blessing because that child is a holy terror."

"Yes, he is." I responded in agreement.

"Miracle, I am going to need you for the next few weeks to come see me. I have something I need to show you. It is very important to the people of this land."

"Whatever, you say Satchel. I will come by this Tuesday. I have the day off."

"That would be great."

"Satchel may I ask you a personal question?"

"Yes, of course."

"How old are you?"

"Miracle I am as old as the old turtle that lives by the river." Satchel said as we both began to laugh.

As we walked up Satchel's front porch stood Elder Dubose, Pastor Lee and Pastor Smith.

"Where you been old Indian? Having the women carry your bags now?" Pastor Lee said.

"Just having a talk with Miracle."

"Miracle, we heard about your beau who married that trollop with her two chicks and a hen. Elder Dubose said.

"My goodness, does everyone know everything around here?" I asked shaking my head.

"Wait till he finds out the truth about being a minister." Pastor Smith said.

"What truth?" I asked.

"All the lies the people put in your head and you thinking you have to appear to be a certain way and yet God just call you for who you are." Pastor Smith replied.

"Let's get in this house and let Miracle get back home." Satchel said.

"Bye" I said as I gave Pastor Smith the bag. Then as I turned to walk away I grabbed Satchel's hand and said "Satchel, I love you."

"Maria, I love you and the people on this land so much more. "

"Satchel, you know my name." I said surprisingly.

And with a kiss on my forehead Satchel said, "I not only know the names of all my blessings, unlike your old beau I know my blessings when I see them. Thank you for carrying my bag."

As I smiled and walked away I could hear the men asking Satchel what did he needed to speak with them about. As the voices became faint I thought where my life would lead me to now.

Chapter 16

Heaven

The next few weeks were still daunting as certain moments I still
cried about David, but Satchel kept me quite busy. He taught me the
places on the reservation where some of the rarest of God's plant
grew. Satchel said he understood why God had to move the people
from the old land. God needed to show him creations yet
unexplored. He taught me the names and uses of those plants.
Satchel tested my knowledge with great diligence and insisted I must
learn my lessons quickly. After about three months, I began to create
some of my own medicines to cure or help ease the burden of
common ailments. For the next six months, though I was exhausted
from all the hard work, Satchel had given me a new outlook on my
life and purpose.

One Sunday while at home it seems as if Yellow Moon went
to wake Satchel from a nap and Satchel had died. When the news
was heard the entire reservation was sad as you heard the sounds of
screams tremble though out our land. That day Elder Dubose
sounded the church bell. We all knew Satchel was old and that he
had been with us people since the beginning. We knew we owed him
a lot more than what we could ever imagine.

It seemed Satchel had spoken to Yellow Moon, Elder
Dubose and Pastor Lee and Pastor Smith regarding his burial. The
next morning the men along with Ted Mims Esquire, Timothy
Cook, Uncle Johnny, and Noah Carter made a raft from the Oak
tree that stood in the center of the reservation. After building it they
laid the hay as high as they could. They dressed Satchel in his Indian
attire he had since he was a young man and place Satchel on the hay.

That evening around six pm all three hundred and seventeen of the reservationists took time from their evening and we watch the elders lay the raft in the river that led to the unknown waters. That day was peaceful and even the wind stood still. As the raft made it to the river the elders lay fire to the hay with a wooden stick. We stood and watch the body float away. As tears flowed from the people's eyes we all had thoughts of how we met Satchel.

As Uncle Johnny began to read the eulogy, Elder Dubose remembered the day he ran off with Ariel only to have to come back to the land empty handed and beaten. He remembered when he made his way back to the old reservation land there stood Satchel with no questions ask and said "Good to see you again, my friend." Pastor Lee remembered how Satchel found him drunk in the city after gambling away the church's money. Satchel bought him back home, cleaned him up, gave him the money to replace what he lost and never told a soul. Pastor Smith remembered when he was eight how Satchel took the sap form a tree vine and place it on his cut leg. Dr. Williams had told his parents he might lose that leg, but Satchel took the vine and covered the leg anyway. Within two weeks Pastor Smith's leg was healed. Ms. Emma remembered when she came to the land after being raped by a white federal officer and Satchel found her at the edge of the reservation. He and "Yellow Moon" took her in their home for one year. One day Satchel asked her to take a walk with him and he stopped in front of a wooden home built by him and his sons, Poncho, Jacob, Sand water and River. He told her this land is where she should stay and that this was her home. She remembered at that moment her life had finally begun. As Uncle Johnny continued to read the eulogy he remembered how

Satchel saw him in the city at a nightclub talking to a girl. The next weekend as he was going to make his way back to the city and walking out the front door, Satchel was waiting and needing to speak with him. Satchel told him how it was the job of a husband to heal his barren wife with his love. Uncle Jonny never cheated on Lela again. Finally Satchel's wife Yellow Moon remembered the first time she saw Satchel. How he had found her in the forest and how she took his hands. These were just a few thoughts people had in their minds of how Satchel made a difference in their lives.

Then I remembered that during his last few months on earth, Satchel had decided to spend some time teaching me the blessings of our land. While tears fell from my face, Yellow Moon came to me and gave me an envelope. I took it and on it was Satchel's handwriting and it read "From Satchel, to my Miracle." I opened the letter and I could not believe the contents. In it was an account of a corporation Satchel had begun from the selling his medicines along with the formulas. Attach was a letter that read:

"Dear Miracle, don't cry because I am gone. You and the people on the land are the responsibility God gave me to heal me from some of the worse pains a man can bear. That is why I lived on this earth for so long. You all gave me a great life. I set up this trust when we came to the new reservation named the "Reservation Inc.". The trust is for the people on this land whom I consider my descendants. You are to continue making profit from the medicines and Dubose, Ted Mims Esquire, Timothy Cook, Pastor Lee and Pastor Smith, Noah Carter along with your Uncle Johnny will help you with the legal and accounting work. I knew this blessing God had given our people would far outlive my years on this earth. The trust states that each year, on the day of my death, profits from the miracles (medicines) found on this land will be divided among my descendants. You are to carry on my work and remember don't cry because I am gone, but smile when you think of the old Indian man. This is from your Chief Elder Satchel."

I closed the letter and place the contents back in the envelope and I knew what I had to do with my life.

Then Uncle Johnny ended the eulogy with these words

"Satchel not only made us better people. He made us better spirits. Good bye, our Indian chief and friend." Then Uncle Johnny took a satchel Yellow Moon had given him. He said Satchel told him when his life ended on earth and began in the sky for the contents in this bag to be divided and given to the families who lived on the reservation. He said it was given to him by our ancestors from the things they had given him when they made their way across the old reservation to freedom. He melted the gold and silver and made nuggets."

Everyone in tears refused as they thought Yellow Moon should keep it all. But she said there was no way she could go against Satchel's wishes. It was at that moment we all saw the rainbow in the sky of many colors and we knew Satchel had made it home to his people he had lost many years ago.

The next day the old turtle by the river was discovered dead by some of the children playing. Rumor had it the turtle was a one hundred and four years of age.